ANOTHER STORY

Chris Orr

My dear wife Hilda and four children Catherine, David, Kerry, and Lisa.

Chapter 1

Ireland 1852

Thomas hit the last nail with one final thud. He wiped the sweat from his brow, before climbing down the ladder. Looking up at the hand-made sign for his new house, he felt a wide mix of emotions inside. 'Mary's House', the sign stated with pride. He turned to look away from the large white stone house to the River Foyle, where the sea waves lapped right up to the garden and, sitting contentedly down on the wooden bench, he stared east at Benevenagh Mountain.

So much had happened in his thirty three years, and now, when he had everything, he couldn't understand the nagging emptiness in his heart. His wedding, five years ago, was such a happy occasion, with the reception being held in Sir William Campbell's estate. William and Maud had pulled out all the stops, despite the sadness of the famine, to make sure they both felt at home. Mary had been still in great distress from her kidnap ordeal in New York but she managed to look striking in her Irish style wedding dress.

Thomas had been still traumatised from losing Christina and his daughter, but his happiness at finally being reunited with his one true love and childhood sweetheart, the beautiful Mary, caused his heart to swell with happiness on that wonderful day.

Their first child, Michael, came a year later, followed two years later by Colleen. They continued to live with Mary's mother till their house in Greencastle was built. The house was magnificent, set in ten acres stretching out on either side of the white stone. A magnificent six bedroomed, three storey house. The River Foyle, at the end of the garden was tidal; a mixture of river and sea water at high tide.

Thomas shivered as the May evening air suddenly woke him from his dreaming and Mary's voice called from the front porch.

'Thomas have you seen Michael?' Mary called.

'Yes, my love. He is here at the side of the house playing in my boat,' replied Thomas sighing.

'Bedtime, Michael. Come now, my wee man,' Mary called. She looked at Thomas, her handsome husband, and felt so proud of the man who came back to marry her after such a sad life in England. Sometimes she could see the pain in his eyes of losing his wife Christina and their daughter in childbirth seven years ago. Even though they had been childhood sweethearts, she wondered how he could have left her and married and an English lord's daughter. Her captivity in New York's sex trade had taken her young life away forever, and even though she had battled her ghosts with an understanding husband, the pain would never go away. They had never talked about each other's past.

Mary was holding Colleen, their two year old daughter, as she moved to Thomas and held his hand. Thomas turned and looked at his best friend and wife of five years and suddenly a warm feeling came over him as he remembered the days of sitting on the hill overlooking Kinnego Bay. He pulled her gently to him and turned her to look at the house with its new sign.

'Will that do ya, girl?' He smiled, pointing to the sign.

Mary stared for a minute, then turned back and smiled, 'It's lovely Thomas, thank you so much. I do not deserve it.'

He paused and dropped his eyes, 'It is I who does not deserve you, my love. I hope I can spend my time on this earth making a happy life for you.'

'My God has blessed me with the kindest man in Ireland, and I have been rescued for a purpose beyond what we can see now.'

'You nearly convince me of this God,' Thomas smiled kindly, lifting his daughter from Mary.

'I don't have to convince you, Thomas, that is His work, and He is doing a pretty good job of it, if you think of where we were seven years ago.'

Thomas stroked Mary's black hair and kissed her gently.

'Ma, look what I have found,' shouted Michael, as he held a frog up by its legs.

Thomas laughed, gave Colleen back to Mary, and rescued the frog, before letting it go by their pond. 'Come on, my young man. It's bedtime.' Thomas swept him up in his strong arms, while Mary watched, before following him up the steps to the front door.

They were eating supper before putting the children to bed, when they heard a carriage pull up at the front door. Thomas leapt to his feet, as the coachman knocked on the door.

'Thomas, my master has collapsed in his house and Lady Campbell asked me to fetch you. Quickly, sir!'

The coachman looked very scared and turned to go back to the carriage.

Thomas grabbed his coat and kissed Mary on the cheek, as he said, 'Maybe it's time to pray to your God, my love. This does not sound good.'

Thomas climbed up beside the coach driver and the two of them sped off to Sir William Campbell's estate two miles away near Moville.

It was getting dark as they sped up the driveway and the house lights were on already in most of the front rooms. Thomas jumped off the coach, even before it stopped at the front door. Lady Campbell was waiting for him at the open door, very upset.

'Oh Thomas, come quickly! He is not good,' she said, trying to remain her usual composed self.

Thomas opened the living room door and found Sir William lying on the sofa, where his wife and staff had placed him.

'Sir William, what have you been doing?' Thomas said, trying to make light of the situation.

Sir William opened his eyes and reached out for Thomas's hand.

'Thomas,' he whispered, 'I'm leaving now.'

'Ah, sure where would you be going at this time of night, William?' Thomas joked, with fear in his voice.

'The pain is bad, son, I know I'm leaving now, so listen to me.' He paused and swallowed as he struggled to speak.

Thomas turned and asked Lady Campbell if she had called the doctor and she replied that the doctor was on his way, but he would be a while.

'Thomas, we owe our lives to you, son,' Sir William choked out. 'These have been the happiest years of my life, since you came back.' He paused again and held Thomas by the arm. 'Can I ask you one last favour, son?'

Thomas now had tears in his eyes as he realised his friend was slipping away. 'I'll do anything for you, sir. There's no need to ask.'

'Look after Maud for me. Please make sure she doesn't do too much.' He gasped.

'Sir William, you are not going anywhere. The doctor is coming for you,' Thomas tried to be brave.

'You were like the son I never had. You are a very special young man.'

'My father would have been so proud of you because of the way you treated Mary and me.' Thomas stuttered. 'She owes her life to you and John. John rescued her from New York, and now I have family, because of your kindness. We will never forget you, sir.'

Maud came over and took William's other hand, while he looked at both of them.

'My life, my only life.' He smiled, as he took his last breath.

Thomas and Maud sat beside him and cried openly. Then John, the estate manager, came in. He had tears in his eyes and, after a few minutes, he put his hand on Thomas's shoulder. 'He has gone now, Thomas,' he said softly and raised Maud up by the arm. 'Come, Lady Campbell the doctor has just arrived.'

Chapter 2

Everyone in Moville and Greencastle turned out for Sir William's funeral. Many people came from Derry and beyond, as he was highly regarded by both communities. Although he was an English landlord, he had treated the local Irish people with great respect and kindness, and had housed over two hundred folks who were homeless and hungry from the famine.

He was buried in the local Church of Ireland cemetery, after a short service. Thomas estimated that there were over six hundred people who tried to get into the small church. The local vicar asked Thomas to say a few words, which left everyone in tears. It was a sad day.

Thomas and Mary escorted Maud back to the house, where they had tea together with John and some of the staff in their kitchen. There was silence, till Maud spoke.

'I deeply appreciate you all coming to William's funeral,' she started, and then paused, wiping a tear from her eye. 'I know how much he meant to all of you, but you must know how much you meant to him, as sometimes he didn't express it too well. Though he grew up in England, this was his home, and he regarded you as his family. Some of you will be worried now that your services will no longer be required, so let me say that that will not happen. I am sure that you will all be fine and I look forward to your help over the next while.'

Maud turned and gave Thomas and Mary a hug. 'Now, my friends, I must try and get some sleep as it has been a long three days.' With that she left the room.

Thomas stood staring at the floor, while Mary lifted some of the dishes off the table.

'Please do not do that,' said one of the kitchen maids, 'we can clear up now.'

'I grew up in a kitchen, Aine, and this is where I feel most contented,' Mary answered, smiling.

'Off you all go and have an evening to rest yourselves. There will be plenty to do in the morning.'

Thomas and Mary were left on their own and stood looking blankly at each other.

'Why Mary?' Thomas asked softly, 'Why do all the good people in my life leave so early?'

Mary didn't answer for she knew that she had nothing to say.

'Four people in seven years. At this rate of going, by the time I am fifty, there will be no one left in Ireland that I know.'

Mary came over and hugged him tightly.

'God gives everyone of us a set time on this earth, my love. We do not know how long we each have.' Mary paused and took Thomas's hands in hers, 'That is why we must make every day count, as you have done, Thomas. We must do that now, together, for our children.'

Thomas stared at Mary and smiled gently. 'Well this God of yours has given me an angel to keep me right.'

'I'm no angel, and one day you will come to know God, as I do, but till then, I know I have a very special man who already has the heart of God.'

John came back in the door holding a steel bucket.

'William's horses are looking for some of the leftovers,' he said sadly.

'Oh John,' Mary said, turning away from Thomas, ' Your heart must be broken today.'

'I should have never let William do so much, Mary. I knew he was struggling to keep up with me.'

'No John, he set himself too high a standard and you had to keep up with him and now you have to carry on what he started.'

'That is what I'm worried about,' sighed John, lifting some of the food and putting it into the bucket.

'Maud will need you even more now, my friend,' Thomas said, patting John on the shoulder.

'We are here for you sir any time you need us.'

'Likewise, Thomas and Mary, you do not even have to ask,' John replied sadly.

They all left the kitchen for the front door.

The month of May gave way to a great Irish June. Thomas kept looking at the old wooden boat that he had built, he wondered when he would have the courage to launch it into the sea. Every time he touched the painted timbers, his heart sank at the memory of his father, Patrick, drowning with Mary's father, Fergal, nine years ago off Kinnego Bay. He still felt guilty for persuading his father to go fishing that day, on his eighteenth birthday. What a beautiful sunny morning that was, when they headed out into the calm Atlantic, not knowing that a storm was brewing. The picture of his father's eyes filled with fear, would never leave him, knowing now that fear was not for himself, but for his son, Thomas.

Thomas was deep in silence when he heard Mary calling him from the front of the house. He turned the corner to find Maud standing beside her carriage, talking to Mary.

'Lady Campbell, good to see you,' he said, shaking hands with her.

'Who are you talking to, Thomas? My name is Maud and always will be.'

'You will always be Lady Campbell to me, Maud,' Thomas smiled.

Maud shook his hand and looked with great sadness into his eyes. 'I will never ever forget you both. There is great hope for this land while people like you live here.'

'What do you mean, Maud, what are you talking about?' Thomas asked, with concern.

'I have decided to go home to England.' Maud paused and looked at Mary. 'There is too much of William in our great house and I can't cope with the pain of losing my best friend. I still have a small cottage on my late father's estate and my sister would be near by. I would have company.' She dropped her eyes to the ground and tears welled up in her eyes. 'I will never settle here.'

'What about the house? It will be very difficult to sell it at this present time, and keeping it up would cost a lot of money,' Thomas replied gently.

Maud turned to Thomas and informed him, 'Thomas, when you gave us back our estate you told us that you would get the deeds transferred back to our name in Dublin. You must have forgotten to do that as you were so busy helping us rebuild the estate. I have discovered the estate is still in your name.' Maud paused and came around to take Mary's hand and put it into Thomas's. 'I give you back your own house, with the blessing of William who wanted that to happen when we were gone.'

'No, Maud, we can't do that. The house is yours for life.' Thomas pulled away from Mary to hold Maud's hands. 'You will need the money from its sale to live on in England.'

'No, sweet Thomas, I will have all I need from my family in England. It's time for me to say goodbye.'

Thomas and Mary were now very upset and could hardly speak.

'Do one thing for me both of you,' Maud paused, with her voice choking, 'Look after John, if you can.' There was silence for a long time then Thomas stepped forward.

'I will look after John, Lady Campbell, you have no fear of that,' Thomas reassured her.

Maud turned and climbed into her carriage with tears streaming down her face. She closed the door and lowered the window.

'God bless you both, till we meet again,' Maud said sadly, staring fondly at them both.

The carriage moved off and left Thomas and Mary, standing arm in arm crying, as they looked after the carriage. Thomas sighed and then said softly, 'How would you feel, my love, if we let John live in the estate? He does most of the work to keep it anyway, and we have a grand new house. What would we need another one for?'

Mary hugged Thomas and answered, 'A man after God's own heart. What a wonderful idea!'

The next day, Thomas slid off his horse, as he approached the door of the estate. The place seemed very quiet as Maud had left with all her possessions the day before. A maid appeared at the front of the house as Thomas hurried towards the front door.

'There's no one here, master,' cried Aine, 'Lady Campbell left yesterday.'

'Yes I know, Aine. Do you know where John is?'

'I saw him at the stables saying goodbye to the horses,' said Aine sadly. 'He was very upset to be leaving.'

'Leaving?' Thomas shouted, with panic in his voice, 'Where is he going?'

'I don't know, master. He seemed very upset after he told us that we would have to leave too.' Aine pointed to the back of the house.

Thomas turned and ran around the back of the house to the stables where John was closing one of the stable doors.

'Where do you think you're going, John?' shouted Thomas.

'Not too sure about that, sir, but I have to go now.'

'Why would you be leaving your own house, John?'

'My house to work in, but the heart is gone now with Maud leaving and there's no work here for any of us now.'

Thomas just stared at him. 'You put your heart, soul, and body into this place. You can't leave now.'

'I did it for a couple who made my life something, when I had nothing,' John replied sadly.

'I know that. No couple had a more faithful servant and friend than you and that's why you cannot leave.'

'Lady Campbell will have to sell the estate, and I'm sure the new owners will choose their own staff.'

Thomas came and stood in front of John and looked him in the eye.

'I forgot to transfer the deeds of the estate to Sir William, so the house still belongs to Mary and me. We promised that we would look after you, so we have decided that you should live here and look after it for your lifetime. I never really thanked you for rescuing Mary from New York, so this is our way of saying thank you now.'

John was speechless, and his eyes were starting to fill with tears. Thomas put his arm around his shoulder as they walked out of the yard to the front of the house.

'I have a new house and more money than any man needs for a lifetime. If we put the estate up for sale, another landlord might buy it, as no one here could afford it, or want it for that matter. It would be a shame to let it go to ruin after all the work that you have done to it. No we have decided that the best option is for you to live in it and make it pay its way again, as I'm sure you could.'

'I can not do that, Thomas. This house was too big for two people, let alone me living here on my own. It would be a terrible waste,' John scolded.

'Well, you'll just have to find yourself a wife and fill it with loads of children, then.' Thomas laughed.

Thomas climbed onto his horse, 'And besides, I am very fussy about the type of neighbour I have beside me.'

'I just don't know what to say. I can't believe you're doing this!'

John just stood and looking at Thomas 'You will have to make it pay, John, to avoid the crown taxes.' Thomas laughed. He turned his horse to ride away. 'I expect an invitation to dinner some time, just to check up on ye.'

John bowed with a great smile. 'Very soon then, Thomas. God bless you.'

Chapter 3

Mary was upstairs dressing Colleen when she heard a strange noise of something being dragged over stones. She picked her child up and went to the window that overlooked the River Foyle. She was shocked at what she saw and ran down the stairs, with so many emotions all at once making her stomach churn. As she opened the front door, Thomas already had the boat at the water's edge and was giving it one last push into the water, helped by Michael, who was squealing with delight. Mary was about to shout at Thomas, but tears were blinding her and no words came out. He had taken two years to build the wooden boat, saying he would never use it and that it was only to remember his dad and Fergal.

Thomas turned and saw Mary watching him. He stared at her, then shrugged his shoulders.

'Come on, Michael, let's have a wee row around the bay,' he said to his son, as he lifted him into the boat. The muscles were tightening in his jaw and his stomach felt sick, but he was determined to beat five years of fear. Mary walked slowly to the water's edge and watched as Thomas rowed the boat around the small bay. Michael was sitting at the back with a smile as big as himself. Thomas never said a word, but suddenly got a flashback of the time he was under the water, when he nearly drowned. He stopped rowing and stared at his son, wishing that his father was there looking at him.

Thomas turned the boat and headed for the shore, where Mary was waiting. The boat scraped onto the shingle and Thomas jumped out, pulling the bow a few feet away from the water. Lifting Michael out of the boat.

'Your father would be so proud of you, Thomas,' Mary said gently, 'and so am I my love.'

'I can never go fishing again, The pain never leaves me,' he sighed.

Mary put her arm around him and walked him back to the house.

Just then John appeared on his huge black horse.

'Good morning, master and ma'am,' he said, smiling.

'Please never call me master, John,' Thomas replied 'I'm only a simple Donegal boy, who made it lucky at many other people's expense. I'm master of none but servant of all.'

'I called by to see what you want to do with our crop land once this year's barley is cut in a few months. Will I do the same again next year?'

'Listen, John. I gave you the whole of the estate to run, not just the house. Now it's up to you to decide what you want to do with it.' Thomas said, firmly.

'All my working life I've had Sir William to tell me what to do. How can I now make those decisions for myself? I have no training.' John seemed nervous.

'John, you had a great trainer. If I didn't believe you could run the estate, then I would have sold it. It's up to you now to make it great again.'

'I'm a simple Donegal man like yourself, Thomas, and feel like I wouldn't be able to take on such a large responsibility.'

'That's the way I felt when I inherited six thousand acres in England, but look how all has worked out for good. Richard has turned it into one of the most prosperous farms in England and lives like a king with his new wife.

John stared at the ground, 'They were so kind to me. I don't deserve any of this, when so many of my people have died from starvation and thousands have fled the country.'

Thomas stroked the head of the horse. 'We have to rebuild this land, and it'll take people like us to do that. The days of sadness are coming to an end and it's time to call the people back to our great country. They will need new crops so that they will never rely solely on potatoes again.'

John turned the horse to leave but turned back to look at Thomas. 'Your kindness has saved so many lives, master, it's a great honour to know you.'

'No, the honour is mine. I wouldn't be here without my Mary, and she wouldn't be here had you not rescued her from New York; We owe you everything.'

John walked the horse away.

The summer was good that year in Ireland, with plenty of sunshine. Parts of the country were still affected by the famine but there was an air of hope again as people learned new farming methods. Farmers were trying to move away from the potato crop and were experimenting with wheat and barley on farms that had arable land. Others were turning to fishing and keeping animals. It would take Ireland twenty years to recover but this was a good start.

Thomas opened a letter as he had breakfast with Mary and the children.

'Oh my goodness!' said Thomas, with excitement, 'It's from Richard. He's going to visit us before August is past with his new wife, Ann!'

'That's great news, Thomas,' answered Mary, pouring the tea, 'I've wanted to meet this famous Richard for a long time. I wonder what his wife will be like.'

'I am sure she'll be every bit as much fun as Richard, my dear friend.

You will love them both.'

Thomas got up from the chair, 'Work to do, my love, the place has to be perfect for my old friend.'

'I am going to visit our mothers today. Can you tell the coachman for me.'

'Tell them I will come soon.' Thomas rushed out the door.

The coach swept into the lane leading to her mother's house and Mary spotted Martha running through the fields. Martha had turned out to be exceptionally pretty and, despite being a slow learner, she had developed into a competent young woman of twenty who could now read and talk in full sentences. 'Ma,' she shouted, 'Ma, Mary's coach is here!' She ran to meet the coach as it reached the front door of Rose's house. As Mary stepped down from the coach, Martha gave her a big hug. 'Mary, Mary are ye home?' she squealed with delight.

'Be careful, Martha. I'm holding Colleen,' Mary laughed.

Rose walked out the door with a brush in her hand. 'I was wondering what all the noise was about. Ah sure, it's great to see ya, Mary.' She took Colleen from Mary. 'Look at the size of me granddaughter! What are ye feeding her on girl?'

Bridget came from the back of the house, carrying a basket of washing. 'Awe look. My favourite daughter-in-law!' She dropped the basket and ran to hug Mary. 'Is my son not with you?' she asked, teasing.

'He's very busy, Ma. 'He sends his love to you.'

'Get in now, till we get the kettle on.' Bridget pushed them in the door.

Rose lifted potato bread off the pan and put it on the table as they sat chatting around the turf fire.

'How's my boy, Mary?' asked Bridget.

'He is good, Bridget, but still finding it hard after losing another friend.'

'That was very sad, very sad indeed. Did they find out what took Sir William so early?'

'Seems the heart gave out on him, Bridget. He was working for the homeless so much.'

'A great man indeed,' Rose interjected, 'Will be sorely missed. Very sad.'

'Is my Thomas happy, Mary? I mean, has he lost the pain of his past?'

'He launched his boat the other day,' Mary said quietly.

'Oh glory, no,' Bridget scolded 'What on earth made him take to a boat that killed his father?'

'He built it over the past two years and I think it's his way of dealing with the loss of Patrick. He promised me he will never go fishing in it, and I believe him.'

Bridget was getting cross, so Rose changed the subject.

Thomas was helping one of his land staff put the last fence post in at the end of his driveway when the taxi coach stopped beside them. A man with a smart tweed coat stepped down. Thomas looked at him with curiosity as he was wearing a strange double pointed hat that reminded him of a man he used to know 10 years ago. The man had asked him to hold a survey pole.

'Excuse me, sir. I'm looking for a young man called Thomas Sweeney,' the man stated, in an English accent.

'Charles?' Thomas shouted in a shocked tone.

The man stood and stared at Thomas, before coming over to shake his hand.

'You must be young Thomas then,' he said, smiling, 'only not such a young lad any more.'

Thomas hugged him.

'What are you doing here, Charles?' Thomas asked.

'I retired a few years ago and I thought I would come back to your beautiful island that I worked in for ten years and see it in a more relaxed way,' Charles said, putting his bag on the ground. 'It was a little difficult to find my way around as the last time I walked everywhere. I couldn't remember your family name so I kept asking local people for a "Thomas".' He paused and chuckled. 'It seems that you have become well known in these parts.'

Thomas lifted his bag. 'I don't know why, Charles, but that's a story for another day. Come with me.'

'How do you, sir,' Mary smiled, 'Excuse the mess. Just trying to keep Thomas in buns.'

'This is Charles, the surveyor man from England who gave me my first job,' Thomas said in a grateful tone.

Mary's face suddenly changed and she started back to her baking. There was silence.

'I have asked Charles to stay with us for a few days.' Thomas came round behind Mary and gave her a hug. The response was cool and awkward and Thomas sensed something was wrong as he said, 'Come on, Charles, I will show you to our guest room.'

They left the room and Mary slammed the dough down on the table, grabbing Colleen and walking out to the front garden.

Thomas showed Charles to his room which had a view of the sea and told him to take his time and then come down for a cup of tea. He found Mary with Colleen by the water's edge.

'What is wrong Mary?' asked Thomas, surprised.

'You brought the man into our house who took you away nine years ago and ruined my life.' Mary answered with anger and tears, 'How could you, Thomas?'

Thomas went very quiet and stood watching her with a sad heart. 'That is true, my love, but look what we have now. We would have none of this if I hadn't gone to England with him.'

'If you hadn't run away with him, Thomas, I wouldn't have gone to New York but would have stayed and had a normal life with my family.'

Mary started to cry, 'You have no idea what I went through in America; no idea of the hell which I live through every day.'

Thomas put his arm round her shoulder but she pulled away. 'Bringing that man into our house brings it all back.'

'He will only stay a few days. It wasn't his fault. It was my own decision to go.'

'It may be good now, but at what cost to us both? It was a bad choice.'

Thomas took Colleen out of her arms and placed her on the sand, giving Mary a big hug.

'Please be civil to him, Mary, for a few days. He could not have been kinder to me when I was a young man with nothing. It wasn't his fault.'

Mary cried hard on Thomas's shoulder, 'I have bad dreams, Thomas, many nights, of the life I had in New York. It won't go away. I'm sorry.'

'You must tell me Mary what happened, in your own words, in your own time. I need to know.'

'You might not want me anymore if I tell you all. It's better you don't know.'

Thomas picked up Colleen and they started walking back to the house. He took Mary by the arm gently and pulled her round to look at him. 'Nothing you tell me will cause me to love you less. I have loved you since I was a wee boy and will love you till the day I die.'

'What about Christina?' she asked sadly, 'Did you love her too?'

'I did, Mary, because I thought I had lost you, but it was a different kind of love. You are my lifetime friend.'

When they went into the kitchen Charles was waiting for them.

'Will you have a cup of tea, sir?' Mary asked politely.

'That would be splendid, ma'am,' replied Charles. 'What a wonderful home you have.'

Thomas spent the next two days showing Charles around the area and estate, talking about the time he graduated as a map surveyor and his time on the English estate.

'Would you ever think of going back to map surveying, Thomas? You were one of the best the ordnance survey company ever had.' Charles asked, wistfully.

'I enjoyed the work very much, Charles, so I don't really count it as work, but there are too many ghosts for me. It was the happiest and the saddest time of my life and, right now, I'm trying to find out who I really am, Charles.' Thomas stopped and picked up a piece of long grass. 'I have everything now, but live every day as if I have nothing.'

Charles took Thomas by the shoulders and looked into his eyes. 'Young man, from the day you agreed to hold the surveying pole for me, I knew there was a great life in store for you, and all that has happened to you was to help you to find out what your destiny is. Live every day as if it's the start of something new and eventually you will find what you are supposed to do.'

Thomas put his arm on his shoulder as they walked back to the house.

Chapter 4

One month later

August was still very warm in Donegal and the countryside looked beautiful as it started to recover from the potato blight and famine. This autumn looked like being the first to actually produce crops in fields where potatoes had failed year after year. Thomas had listened to Richard's advice and introduced new farming methods that had made the English estate so successful.

Richard and his new wife were due to arrive tomorrow and Thomas and Mary were busy making sure the house and gardens were ready. Thomas was painting the barn door at the north side of the house when John arrived on his horse.

'Good day, Thomas,' he called, as he dismounted. 'Good to see you working sir.'

'I'm not "sir", John, and if you call me that again I'll steal your horse and send him to the knackers.' Thomas laughed, leaving down the paintbrush. 'I have a spare brush if you want to give me a hand, or is that beneath you now that you live in such a fine house?'

John just looked at him and smiled. 'I need your opinion,' he started, as he walked towards the barn. 'Some of the locals that Sir William took in when things were bad are wanting to go back to their cottages and farms but can't afford to pay rent. We have only about twenty families left.' He paused and stared at the ground. 'I was thinking what I might do with them.'

'Go on John,' Thomas responded. 'This sounds interesting.'

John got nervous and sat down on the old wooden bench, 'The estate owns about forty cottages spread out all over the area here, and half were abandoned during the famine when folks died or could no longer pay their rent.' He looked up at Thomas, 'As you were generous to me, I was thinking I might do the same for the families that need a house.'

There was silence between them before Thomas answered, 'Now why would you be asking me, John?'

'You still own the estate, and it would be up to you if you didn't mind losing the potential income from the cottages.'

'I gave you the estate to run and told you to do with it what you want. The income is for you to decide how to manage.'

'Oh my goodness! Are you serious?' John spluttered, standing up.

'Yes my friend, it's all yours, but the bad news is that you will be responsible for the crown taxes if it becomes profitable again,' Thomas laughed.

John moved to his horse, 'You're always helping other people, Thomas. I believe God has you here for this time.'

'Everyone mentions God to me, as if I should know Him.'

John mounted his horse. 'You should, as you live like a man who already does. I'm off to tell the folks they can have the houses back, thanks to you.'

Thomas stared after him as he rode down the lane. Mary came out of the side door with Michael by the hand.

'What did John want?' she asked, moving over to look at the newly painted barn.

'He is spending too much time with generous people, and is going to give twenty cottages away to the folks that Sir William took in.'

'He's a man after God's own heart then,' Mary said, looking pleased with herself.

'If you mention God again to me today, I'll move you closer to Him.'

Thomas laughed, and picked up the paintbrush.

Thomas stood at the bottom of the lane waiting for the taxi coach to arrive from Derry. It was lunchtime and he was hungry, having missed breakfast, because he had so many jobs to do before Richard and his wife arrived. He was thinking back to the first day he and Richard arrived at the estate in England to spend a year doing a private land survey. Richard was like a wee boy then and the two of them were trying to keep their excitement from showing too much when they were introduced to Lord Shrewsbury. How life changed so rapidly for them both, when he fell in love with the Lord's daughter, Christina. Tragedy had ruined their honeymoon when the lord was killed in a coach crash and, a year later, Christina died in childbirth. Thomas had inherited the entire six thousand acre estate, which he handed over to Richard to run when he decided to come home to Ireland.

Thomas's thoughts were interrupted by the clatter of the coach approaching.

He was almost dancing with excitement as Richard and his wife stepped down from the coach. Richard ran to Thomas and left his wife to talk to the coach driver.

'Thomas, my old codger,' shouted Richard, 'How the hell are you?'

Thomas and Richard hugged for so long that Thomas thought his ribs were going to break. 'Richard, my old friend,' Thomas laughed, 'What a day this is!'

Richard pulled away and turned to introduce his wife. She was slim and tall, dressed expensively in the typical English fashion of the time.

'May I introduce my wife, Ann,' Richard smiled.

Thomas took her hand and kissed it, bowing slightly. 'My goodness, Richard! I told you to find yourself a pretty wife but I did not expect you to find the prettiest girl in England!'

'I've heard so much about you, Thomas,' Ann said gently. 'In fact my husband mentions your name so often, that I felt I knew you,' she laughed. 'I am looking forward to finding out if Richard's stories are exaggerated.'

'Come now both of you,' said Thomas, as he lifted Ann's case. 'I won't be telling any tales, as Richard is quite well able to make them up for himself,' he laughed.

Mary was waiting for them at the front door with the two children by her side.

'This is my wife, Mary,' Thomas said proudly, and my two children, Michael and Colleen.

Mary held out her hand to Ann, but Ann gave her hug. 'Mary, you are so pretty,' Ann said, 'it's no wonder Thomas left England to marry his true love.'

Richard stepped forward and bowed, taking Mary's hand. 'It's my immense privilege to meet the woman who stole my best friend away from me. Now I see why.'

They all went inside to the huge living room that Thomas had designed as an exact replica of the estate house in England.

'There was I thinking you were living in poverty, my friend,' said Richard, laughing. 'Now I see that giving up living with me certainly didn't take the English lifestyle out of you.'

'Stop now, Richard. It would be hard to give up anything after all the fun we had,' Thomas laughed.

During the next two days Thomas showed Richard and Ann around the Inishowen peninsula with its golden beaches and some of the best scenery in Ireland. At dinner that night Thomas announced that he would take Richard on his own to his favourite place, Kinnego Bay, where his life started. Mary agreed to take Ann to meet her mother.

Thomas took two horses, as he left the coach for Mary and Ann. They headed out towards Moville, before turning north for the dirt track that led over the mountain to Kinnego Bay.

'There was I, thinking you were missing life in the West Country, Thomas,' said Richard, as the horses climbed the steep hill. 'I can see now, in this beauty, why you wanted to come home.'

'It's pretty today, but this place has been through five years of extreme sadness with the failure of the potato crop,' Thomas sighed. 'They say over a million people have died in Ireland and nearly as many have left for better shores – and it's not over yet.'

'I haven't seen much arable land yet. It's not hard to know that they need help here.'

'I have got some of the farmers to try your idea of crop rotation and moving away from potatoes, but the people lived here on potatoes for centuries, so it's very hard for them to change.'

It took two hours for them to ride over the mountain, till at last they came to Kinnego Bay.

Richard stopped and looked down at the bay for a long time, then shook his head. 'This must be one of the most beautiful places on earth Thomas.'

Thomas climbed down from the horse and tied the reins to a small tree. Richard followed him. 'It's too steep for the horses, and we need to walk anyway.'

Thomas stopped at the corner. 'This is where Mary and I used to sit and dream.'

'Do you not still do that?' Richard asked softly.

Thomas turned and looked at him with great pain in his eyes. 'This was my favourite place in all the world till my father and Mary's father drowned down there.' He pointed to the rocks. 'It's hard to believe that such beauty holds such sadness.'

The two of them walked down to the beach in silence; a silence where close friends don't need to say anything.

'They found me here on the beach nearly dead,' Thomas sighed. 'Some days I wish I had drowned with them.'

'I would have never met my best friend if you had. In fact, I would still be working in a dusty old office in Southampton and living as a boring old bachelor.'

'I know, my friend, but look at the cost of what we have now,' Thomas sighed.

Thomas bent down and picked up a stone and threw it into the sea. 'You chose well, Richard. Ann is an amazing lady, and I'm sure you will have a lifetime of happiness, you old codger.'

'Less of the "old", son,' laughed Richard. 'Come and show me more wonders of this land.'

They walked back up the steep path to the horses. It was dinner time when they arrived back at the house, both saddle sore from the many miles they had covered.

'The wanderers have returned, Ann,' Mary said, as she started to put out their dinner in the kitchen.

The next day, Thomas took both of them to see Sir William's estate.

'My jolly goodness,' Richard gasped, 'This is almost as good a house as your English estate.'

'Everything I did was a copy of what you have already done in England.' Thomas said, smiling. 'How is my property going these days?'

'It's doing so well that I'm worried the owners will put me out and claim the house back for themselves.'

'Can't happen, as I made a legal contract with them when the lord died. I gave the title back to his brother, Henry, on condition that, not only would I have a large income in perpetuity, but also that the estate would be managed by you. You turned it from a loss-making mess into one of the most valuable properties in the west of England and they will hardly risk losing their income on such a valuable asset. No, my friend, you will be there with your lovely wife for a very long time.'

John appeared from the side of the house.

'John, this my old friend, Richard, and his wife, Ann.' Thomas shouted, as John walked towards them.

'It's an honour to meet the famous Richard,' said John, shaking hands with them. 'I hear your name mentioned ten times a day.'

'I'll tell you all later, John,' laughed Richard.

John showed them around the house and gardens.

'What about the political situation in Ireland, John?' asked Richard, when they were out of earshot of the others. 'The census taking place is going to show Westminster just how tragic your famine has been.'

John dropped his eyes to the ground. 'There is growing discontent in Ireland about our land being governed by London, and if the feeling spreads, with a poor response from government, then it doesn't bode well for our wee land.' John looked nervous, as he didn't want Thomas hearing their conversation. He continued, 'Sometimes I think Thomas has become more English than Sir William Campbell, who owned this estate. He'll never let anyone say a bad word about the English.'

'The English made him, and he will never get over the death of his wife, and, to be honest, we are not the worst of people,' Richard smiled.

'Many English people, also, are angry at the way our government responded to the famine'

Their brief conversation came to an end when the others joined them at the fountain in the front garden.

'This fountain reminds me of something,' Richard said sadly.

Thomas turned and looked at him with great sadness in his face, 'It's a replica of the one we have in our estate, Richard.'

No more was said, as Richard remembered that it was Christina who designed the fountain, and he sensed Thomas was getting uncomfortable. Mary looked at Richard and was about to ask more about the fountain in England when Richard suggested that John show them the stables.

August was giving way to September when it was time for Richard and Ann to leave.

Mary and Ann had got on very well as they both had come from a working class family like Richard. He had met Ann at the local pub and fell in love very quickly. She had no idea that Richard lived in a huge estate house.

They all stood waiting for the taxi coach to come and Thomas's heart was heavy. Richard's visit had brought his past back with great sadness. Part of him was buried in England and it added to the feeling of emptiness he felt every day that he tried to cover up by working at new projects.

Thomas and Richard stood aside from Mary and Ann. 'I still have an urge to become an engineer and design stuff, Richard, and do what my father was good at,' Thomas sighed. 'And to do that, the only place for me to be is in America.'

Richard looked with great concern at his friend. 'Oh, Thomas, my friend. It's just because of everything you've been through. You have everything here, and you have made such a difference to so many people's lives.'

Thomas shrugged his shoulders. 'Why do I have an emptiness inside me then? It won't go away, and every day I wake up thinking, 'Why am I on this earth?''

Ann and Mary approached them as the coach appeared from Greencastle. Richard hugged Thomas tightly and whispered, 'You are one of the greatest men God put on this earth, and I'm sure you'll find your purpose if you wait for it, but, in the meantime, keep doing what you are doing, as so many people need it. Come and visit your old home sometime. It might help put the ghosts to rest.'

Thomas pulled back and looked Richard in the eye. 'I'll never have a friend like you, Richard. Think about coming to live here some day.'

'Not a hope,' Richard laughed, 'I'm hoping if I stay on the estate that they might give me a title to go with it.'

They all hugged before boarding the coach. As the coach disappeared, Mary turned and looked sadly at Thomas and asked, 'Who designed the fountain Thomas? It wasn't you was it?'

Thomas stood transfixed, staring at the road, till he felt his eyes misting. 'It's in the past, my love,' he said, taking her hand, 'Time to go home.'

Mary pulled away and lifted Colleen into her arms. 'It was Christina who designed the fountain, wasn't it? Do you still love her?' she asked softly.

'Come, Michael,' replied Thomas, as he took his son's hand, 'let's launch the boat again.'

Mary walked behind them with tears in her eyes.

Chapter 5

8 years later 1860

All of Mary and Thomas's family were gathered in the living room as Mary lit the candles on the birthday cake in the kitchen. Thomas was sitting at the table with his son, Michael, who was now thirteen, working on the design of a new machine. Colleen, now twelve, was twirling about in front of her two grandmothers, Bridget and Rose, showing off her new dress. Martha. now thirty, had grown into a very pretty young woman, and was busy decorating a new tapestry that she had made out of dried flowers.

Mary appeared at the door with the cake and the candles lit. Thomas was thirty-six today. The responsibility of the last eighteen years showed on his handsome face and had caused his hair to turn grey at the sides. Mary place the cake on front of him, kissing him gently on the lips. 'Happy birthday, my darling husband,' she smiled.

'Thank you all so much.' Thomas stood up and bowed towards them. 'How very kind of you all.'

Mary cut the cake and handed out a piece to everyone, before Thomas excused himself and left with Michael. 'We have a wee job to do before it gets dark. Thank you, and please excuse us.'

Thomas and Michael went out to the boat with the drawings they had been working on and began doing some measurements.

The party was ending and their folks were getting ready to get on the carriage.

'Thomas, your mother is leaving,' called Mary.

Thomas left Michael and walked over to the carriage to kiss his mother and hug Rose.

'I'll come and see you shortly,' he said, as he helped them up the step into the carriage.

When Thomas came into the house it was dark and the children were in bed and Mary was washing the last of the party dishes. Thomas came behind her and put his arms around her waist. 'Thank you, my sweet Mary, for such a nice surprise for my birthday.'

Mary turned and kissed him on the lips, then stepped back. 'Is there something wrong, my love?' she asked, with concern in her eyes.

'Now what would make you feel like that?' Thomas replied softly

'I know by now, Thomas, when you kiss me, how much you mean it,' she said sadly.

Thomas looked into her eyes for a long time in silence, wondering how he was going to have the courage to tell her what was on his heart.'

'Mary, do you remember my father, Patrick?' he paused, and looked down at the floor. 'He was a great inventor, only life took him away before he could develop or patent any of his clever ideas.'

Mary was looking increasingly anxious as what might be coming next. 'He always encouraged me to do the same thing, and it has been my life long dream to do that. I lie awake at night thinking of new machines that would make life so much easier for people, and wake up feeling frustrated. I now realise that it's this very thing that has been causing the emptiness in my heart all this time. I know I was born to help people, not by what I am doing here, but by making machines that will make life easier for them.'

Mary wiped her hands on her apron and moved towards the cupboard to hang the cups on hooks. Without looking back at Thomas, she said, 'And what does this all mean to us?'

Thomas waited a long time, then quietly said, ' The only way I can fulfil my dream is to go to America.'

Mary felt the colour drain from her face. Sitting down on one of the kitchen chairs, she looked up at Thomas in disbelief, unable to speak.

'I know how that would be difficult for you, but we could avoid New York and live in the country.' Thomas was rubbing his hands with nerves and sat down opposite Mary. He continued, 'it's the land of opportunity and new beginnings. There's nothing in this wee island but pain and misery, and it's only going to get worse till we get our own government.'

'So what would we do here without you?' Mary asked, anxiously.

'I mean for us all to live there for a while; maybe two or three years.'

'Have you any idea what you asking us all to do, Thomas, just because you want to fulfil a selfish dream? I will never go back to that evil place – nor will my children!'

Thomas knew it was time to go to bed, and so he left Mary without another word.

'Never means never!' she shouted after him.

The next few days were very quiet in the house, as Mary wouldn't talk to Thomas, and he was too scared to bring up the subject again. Winter was coming in fast that year and with it strong winds and rain battered the house, meaning Thomas couldn't get out of Mary's way.

A few days later, when the children were in bed and Mary was sitting by the turf fire, Thomas came in and sat down beside her on the sofa. He turned to her and said, in a very forceful way, 'Now, Mary, we are not moving from here till you tell me everything that happened to you in New York, and I mean everything. I am your husband. How am I to look after you when you won't tell me about your pain. It stops tonight or I will leave here in the morning and never come back.'

Mary turned and looked at him and knew that he meant what he said. 'Get me a glass of brandy, please,' she asked in a pathetic tone.

Thomas was shocked. 'You don't drink,' he said, 'Why do you want a drink?'

Mary jumped up and went to the dresser and poured herself a large brandy and gulped it straight down. 'Right, Thomas, you want to know. Well, I will tell you, but you'd better be ready.'

It was two hours later, with both of them in tears, that Mary finished telling Thomas of her kidnap and of being forced into the sex trade in New York. They talked for a long time, also, about Christina, and Thomas felt afterwards like a great weight had been lifted off his shoulders.

They both hugged like never before and eventually fell asleep in each other's arms.

Thomas had a big breakfast ready for Mary when she woke up. She stumbled into the kitchen and sat down opposite Thomas. She smiled, 'That was the first time I've ever been drunk in my life, and it will be the last.'

Thomas reached across the table and took her hands in his, 'I love you more than ever, Mary, and by telling me your story last night, you have released me from Christina and my life in England.'

She stroked his hands, 'Can you take me to Kinnego Bay today?'

'In this weather?' replied Thomas with surprise.

'Yes, in this weather, my love, I want to start over.' She smiled at him and felt like her heart was bursting with love for her husband.

'Thank you for telling me about Christina, my love. She must have been a very sweet girl.'

'She was, very special, but God wanted us to be together and I realise now it was you that I really love.'

'When did you start believing in God?'

'Last night, when you told me your story. There were too may coincidences to be just chance. Your God was looking after you.'

'Oh, Thomas, God loves you so much.' She came round the table and gave him a great big hug.

Over the next two weeks there was a completely different atmosphere in the house. It was as if Thomas and Mary had fallen in love for the first time. Thomas couldn't stop thinking that suddenly he had a complete change of direction by believing in a God that he had blamed for everything that had gone wrong in his life. Now it was if he didn't need answers anymore and that, if he trusted in this God that he didn't really know before, then everything would work out in the end. Mary walked as if she had been given her whole life back, and the pain of the past was now gone, even though it was not forgotten.

Thomas dismounted from his horse at John's front door and rang the old bell cord on the right side. He heard the old bell ring deep in the house that he loved so much. John came to the door and was delighted to see Thomas.

'Well, master. How good it is to see you on this cold October day. Come in to the heat quickly.

'The house is looking so well, John. You have done William proud. He'd be so delighted to see you kept everything in such good shape.'

'As long as I live this house will be a memorial to two of the finest people to set foot on this island. Maybe one day my heart will mend,' John said sadly, 'God has blessed me beyond all I could ever expect.'

'I have come to know your God, John.' Thomas said, with a big smile.

John was silent and looked in disbelief, till he could see that Thomas was serious, 'That's great news indeed! He'll never let you down.'

Thomas moved to the big fire burning with huge logs and warmed his back, before turning to John, 'I need a big favour – in fact, I need a few favours.'

'Anything you ask I will try and do for you, as always.'

'I would like to take my family to America for a few years. Ever since I was a young boy, my late father encouraged me to invent things, and the only way I can fulfil my dream is to go the land where dreams come true.'

John was very quiet and a look of shock and panic flashed across his face, before he stuttered

'That's some decision, sir. And would Mrs Sweeney feel the same way?'

'I'm working on that, and as long as we stay away from New York, I believe I may be able to persuade her.' John moved from the fire to the window overlooking the gardens. 'I've been quietly doing some research and I believe I have enough money and new ideas to make a new business there.'

'What can I do for you, sir,' John asked quietly.

'When you rescued Mary, you made contact with someone that Sir William knew, and I was wondering if the same man could help us get into the country.'

'The friend of Sir William was a New York policeman called O'Hare. He was very helpful, but a busy man, and he may not still be there but I will send a cable to him and see what I can do. What else can I do for you, sir?'

Thomas turned and looked at John with sad eyes. 'I need someone to look after my house for a few years and look after my family at Kinnego Bay. It's a very big responsibility to ask anyone but there is no one else in the world I would trust with either task.'

John had tears in eyes and could hardly speak, 'You will come back?'

Thomas came and put his hands on John's shoulders, looking at him with eyes which were also tearful. 'I promise you, my friend, three years will be the longest I'll be gone. If my plans go well then I we will return.'

They hugged, and Thomas left the house and rode home.

John stood at the front door staring down the lane wondering if life would ever return to normal, before getting the coach to drive into Derry.

Chapter 6

Christmas Day of 1860 was a subdued time. Thomas had brought his mother, Mary's mother and Martha, to spend the day with them. Everyone had been told that Thomas and Mary would leave for New York in January. The arguments had all been had, and even Mary had become used to the idea, if only just to keep Thomas happy. John was invited too, as he was still living on his own in the estate house. Dinner was over, and they were all sitting relaxed by the big fire.

'No sign of any "Mrs" yet?' Thomas asked John, with a mischievous grin.

John just smiled, 'Now why would I tell you if there was, Thomas? You would just be offering me advice all day.'

Thomas laughed, 'Yes I suppose I would, and perhaps that advice might not be the best. Richard is the man to ask. He seemed to have had no trouble getting a wife.'

'Yes, but when all the locals think that he owns six thousand acres there would, naturally, be a long queue of eligible ladies waiting for him.'

'That's true,' he conceded, and took a long drink of mulled wine, 'but apparently Ann had no knowledge of this before she agreed to marry him.'

'He's a very clever man. To turn a loss-making estate into profit in two years is some achievement.'

Thomas smiled, 'It might just have something to do with my idea of flooding the valley and starting an electricity-generating dam on it, and selling off two hundred acres to the new town being built on the north end of the estate.'

'What mad scheme have you in mind for America? Are you going to flood some more valleys there?'

Thomas smiled at him and sat down beside Mary. 'No, I have been doing a lot of research and discovered that all the new railways that are being built are using British steel and train engines. I have looked at them and reckon I can design and make better ones in America.'

Everyone went very quiet in the room and looked at Thomas as if he had lost his mind. Mary was the first one to speak.

'Will that require a very large sum of money, and people with engineering backgrounds?' she asked.

'I believe I have enough money to start a small works in the country, and would expect it to grow rapidly.' Thomas replied, standing up and going over to Michael who was playing with his new toy boat. 'It's just one of my ideas, but we will see how things go.'

Mary changed the subject by asking, 'More wine anyone?'

10th January 1861

Thomas and Mary had already said goodbye to their parents the day before, so there were only John and some of his staff gathered to see Thomas and Mary and their two children board the coach for Derry.

'I expect to see this estate thriving by the time we get back, and hopefully you'll be married and starting a family.' Thomas said, as he helped them all onto the coach. The driver had put their huge luggage cases on the roof and back and the coach looked very unstable.

'I hope your ship is more stable looking than that carriage, and yes, I'll work hard for you and Sir William to make this pay,' John answered, trying to keep back the tears.

Thomas came over and hugged him. 'Look after the locals, John, they need a lot of help to recover from the blight.'

'I will master, and do write often, so I can sleep at night.'

'God bless you, my friend.' Thomas turned and climbed into the coach as it moved away.

The wind and rain were beating down on the harbour as their coach approached the ship. Mary's stomach was in knots as she remembered boarding a similar ship in 1843, bound for the same harbour. That time she was on her own, with a broken heart, as Thomas had gone to England with a strange man and had made no contact with his family. To provide for her family, who had lost her father in a fishing boat tragedy, she felt she had no option but to seek work in New York, to where many Irish people were already travelling. The nice man who had helped her on board the long journey then introduced her to important people when the ship docked. Her heart sank as she remembered being taken to a nice house, then locked up and forced into prostitution. She was almost sick with fear as Thomas took her by the hand to help her down from the coach.

'It will be all right, my love,' Thomas reassured her, 'No one will ever touch you again.'

Mary helped Michael and Colleen get their things, as the coachman, helped by dockers, lifted their cases and brought them on board. A ship's officer, in a smart uniform, met them at the top of the gangway.

'May I welcome you aboard, Mr and Mrs Sweeney. My steward will show you to your cabins.'

There were only a small number of private cabins on the ship as most people fleeing Ireland could only afford to sleep in large shared open rooms.

'Thank you, sir,' replied Thomas, 'How long does it normally take to make the crossing across the Atlantic?'

'With our new ships powered by steam and sail sir, we can do the crossing in about four weeks – unless we hit bad weather,' replied the officer, looking very proud of his ship.

'The weather doesn't look too good out there,' Thomas remarked, as he took Mary's hand.

'It will be a bit choppy tonight, sir, but the forecast is good for the rest of the voyage, considering it's January.'

The steward escorted them to the small first class area of the ship, where they found their cabins.

'This is just a bit better than the last time I did this journey, Thomas.' Mary hugged him as they stood in the middle of their cabin. 'A lot has changed in eighteen years.'

'For the better, my sweet Mary, and only can get better.' Thomas kissed her hard on the lips, before they were interrupted by Michael and Colleen.

'Why do I have share a cabin with Colleen?' complained Michael.

'It's not ideal at your ages,' replied Thomas, gently, 'There were only two cabins available and it's only for a few nights. Colleen, you can change and wash in here, so you will only be sleeping in the same room.' Thomas grabbed and hugged them under each of his strong arms. 'We will find a grand house for you in America, though it might take awhile, so try and be as kind to each other as you are at home.'

It was getting dark as the ship slipped out of its berth in Derry and started the one hour journey to the mouth of the River Foyle. Despite the cold and wet, Mary insisted on standing on the small outside deck to see the ship passing their house at Greencastle.

'Three years. Promise me that,' Mary said sadly as she watched

Donegal slipping out of sight behind them.'

'I promise, my love. Then we will return and settle at home for ever.'

'I have to do this for my father or I'll die with the guilt of missing his and my dream.'

'I know, my love. I will be beside you and God will direct us.'

The first night at sea was quite rough, as the officer had told them, but the rest of the journey across the Atlantic was calm. Michael was bored as, once he had walked around the ship a few times, there was little for him to do but sit and help his father design new things. Colleen was content to sit and dream with her mother as to what life would be like in the new world.

Three weeks later, everyone became excited when the ship's horn sounded to let them know that land had been sighted, and the passengers rushed to the open decks, even though it was very cold. There was a light spattering of snow. Mary was sick in her stomach as she looked at the New York skyline.

Thomas and Mary left the ship by the front gangway as people were pushing themselves to the rear to get off the ship. The harbour looked drab in the evening light, even with the light covering of snow. There were rows of horse drawn carriages waiting to take the immigrants to their different destinations. For those lucky enough to have relations or friends, the start of their new life would be a lot easier than those who came on their own, as Mary had discovered in 1843.

The first thing that Thomas noticed was the smell. 'What's the reek?' he asked quietly, helping her down off the gangway.

'That's the city. I remember it well,' Mary replied, shivering in the cold.

'Come on, my love. Let's find Lieutenant O'Hare and get out of here.'

Just then a tall man in a suit wearing a trilby hat and long overcoat came up to them.

'Would you be Mr and Mrs Sweeney?' he asked, smiling, 'I am Alfred O'Hare.'

'Hello, sir. Nice to meet you, though I thought you would be in uniform.'

'Just retired, Mr Sweeney, and waiting to join the army. I have a young man with me who will help you with your cases. We need to get you out of the cold.'

'Please, Lieutenant, call me Thomas, and this is my wife, Mary, and my two children, Michael and Colleen.'

'I am very glad to meet you all, but amazed – especially to meet you, Mary! I believe things were very difficult for you here before", he blurted out, before realising what he'd just said. He helped them up into his carriage, before climbing in beside them.

Mary looked at the floor and felt very cold. She took Thomas's arm in hers.

'Before I left the police tried to break the gangs that were kidnapping folks off the ships, but they always found ways to beat us, and sadly, it's still going on.' He knocked on the carriage wall and the driver moved off. 'We need to get through this part of the city before it gets dark as there are some pretty unsavoury people about here at night.'

The coach drove fast down endless streets of warehouses, and then shops, before coming to a more residential part of New York. Thomas noticed that coaches on rails were being pulled by horses, and that there were a lot of train stations along their route.

'We'll be fine now, folks,' O'Hare said, laughing, 'You are all welcome to my great city.'

'It's very kind of you to do all this for us, Lieutenant. We deeply appreciate your kindness,' said Mary kindly.

'I was very shocked to hear of my friend, William, dying suddenly like that.' He shook his head and looked sadly out of the coach window. 'He was exceptionally kind to me when I was a young man back in England, and he helped me get into the English police, even though I was from Ireland. That was my first step in coming here.'

'He was kind to everyone, sir, right up to the end, and it probably cost him his life,' replied Thomas sadly.

'How was that, Thomas?' asked O'Hare frowning.

'All the people who were made homeless by the famine; he found accommodation for them and he and his wife fed them at their house for over a year. The doctor thinks it was the stress of caring for nearly two hundred people that gave him a heart attack.'

'I always had intended to go home to Ireland and see him, but my job here in the city got so busy once so many of you Irish folks started arriving.'

The conversation changed when Michael got very excited to see a steam train pulling a long row of carriages.

'It's another half hour's drive to your new house, Mary,' O'Hare said gently. 'It's in the country, as you requested, but only ten minutes from the nearest town, so you can have the best of both worlds.'

'Thank you so much, Lieutenant, I hope we have not put you to too much bother.'

'Not at all ma'am. My wife and I have just moved to the town, so we'll be neighbours, I guess.'

'Lieutenant, you said you left the police and you are going to join the army?' queried Thomas.

'Yes, sir. I'm afraid you have come to America at a bad time.' He paused and lowered his voice so as not to scare the children, 'War is about to break out here, and I have decided it's a cause worth fighting for.'

Thomas looked alarmed, but tried to keep it from Michael and Colleen. 'What war, sir? Fighting whom?'

O'Hare looked very sad and shrugged his shoulders, 'Ourselves, Thomas, ourselves.'

Thomas and Mary looked very anxious, so O'Hare said he would chat to them in a few days and tell them all.

The coach pulled up at the front door of their new home. The snow had stopped and the moon was shining blue light onto the bushes on the front garden. It was a typical American grand house, with a winding driveway to a front porch with white pillars. The front door was open with a large happy looking housekeeper waiting for them.

The Lieutenant helped take their cases into the house and told them that he would come back and see them in a few days, just to make sure they had everything they needed.

The house was very warm, with two big open fires downstairs and a small open fire in each bedroom upstairs. It was not long before they were all asleep.

Chapter 7

Thomas was up first the next morning as he longed to get stuck into his new life in America. The sun was shining and the light snow had melted. He spent the next hour walking around the house and grounds, and was surprised to see there was very little he had to do. The house was sitting in four acres, with mature trees all around the garden. There was nearly an acre of ground at the back which was covered in fruit trees and vegetable patches. The air was crisp and clear as he took deep breaths, with a mixture of fear and excitement. This was a huge decision he had made, that would affect his whole family, yet he could not hide the excitement of new beginnings. He turned the corner at the east side of the house and there was Michael standing on the front porch, staring out in front of him.

'Is this really ours, Da?' he asked, quietly.

'For now, son,' Thomas sighed, 'I have put a three year limit on us staying here. It wouldn't be fair to keep you all away from your family and life at home.'

'I have little to do at home, Da. What will I do here?' he shrugged his shoulders and walked down the steps to meet his father.

'Well, son, you have a few more years to do at school, as I don't want you ending up like me.'

'You did alright, Da,' sighed Michael, 'without any school.'

'That was a different time, Michael, and I was exceptionally lucky to get into the ordnance survey office on a training scheme, whereas now I would have to have a basic education first.'

'I want to work with you, Da, making things.'

'I know, son, but first we must learn a whole new way of life and learn to fit in with very different folks than back home.'

Michael was silent and kicked a few of the stones on the driveway. Just then Mary and Colleen appeared at the front door, 'There you two are. I was wondering why you weren't down for your breakfast.' They all went inside, where a cook had prepared their first breakfast in their new home.

'The city seems much busier than when I was here eighteen years ago,' Mary said, to make conversation.

'It's the biggest and busiest town in America,' replied Thomas, finishing his tea and toast. 'There are plenty of opportunities for people who want to try new things.'

'The people all speak funny,' chipped in Michael.

'I like the clothes,' added Colleen.

They all stopped when they heard a carriage enter the driveway. 'Who would that be so early?' Mary said, as she rose from the table with dishes in her hand.

Thomas went to the front door, where Lieutenant O'Hare was already walking towards him.

'Good morning, sir. Welcome to a warmer day in New York,' he said, smiling and holding out his hand to Thomas. 'Thought you might like a quick tour of the neighbourhood so you don't get lost in this big world.'

'Sounds good, Lieutenant. I'll let Mary know I'm away for a while.'

'I would be very pleased if you'd call me Alfred,' Lieutenant O'Hare shouted after him.

The trip on the coach lasted two hours, as Alfred took them down every country lane and showed Thomas many neighbouring properties that were hidden away. 'New York is full of very rich people,' started Alfred, as he pointed to some huge houses in the midst of magnificent gardens. 'It has its poor areas like Five Points, but most of it's very rich.'

Thomas was quiet, as he tried to take it all in. 'I didn't come here for the money, Alfred, as I am already wealthy, but I came because I want to invent new ways of doing things that will help people.'

'Thomas, take my advice, sir. If you want to succeed here, you will have to fit in very quickly.

That means, for the first while, you will need to meet the right people. The wealth is controlled here by a few and they do not take kindly to immigrants, no matter where they are from. If you want to invent new products, then you need to spend time looking at what is here already, then finding the person who might help you make that product happen. You have given yourself a very short window of two to three years, so be prepared to go home to Ireland disappointed.'

Thomas turned and looked at him for a while. 'What is this war you talked about?'

'Our President Lincoln, who wants a united America, wants to free the slaves in the South. Many of the huge farms in the South have black slaves that harvest their cotton and grain for them, that makes the farms highly profitable. Many of the slaves have been there all their lives and, while many of them want to be free, not all do. The problem is that there are many business people in the North here who are connected to the cotton industry in the South, so not everyone here in New York wants a war. It will be Americans fighting Americans – even families against their own - so feelings are running high on both sides. It may not happen yet, but every week it looks more and more likely. I was approached by a general in the Union Army, and he convinced me to retire from the police and take a position as an officer. it's unlikely that I would actually be on the front line, but I could be asked to develop a defence force for New York should the war come to our door.'

'Not a good time to arrive in New York then, Alfred?' sighed Thomas.

'Quite the opposite,' laughed Alfred, patting him on the back, as they alighted from the carriage. 'If you are an inventor, then now is your time to invent something for war.'

They were back at the front door and Thomas thanked Alfred for his kindness.

'Next week, Thomas, I will introduce you to people who matter and who can make things happen for you, but, till then, enjoy meeting your neighbours. You never know when you will need them, my friend.'

The carriage sped down the stone driveway as Thomas looked on.

Thomas came into the huge kitchen and found Mary crying, as she baked some bread for the day. He went up behind her and gave her a big hug. 'What is wrong, my love?' he asked, tenderly.

'I don't know, Thomas. I don't know.' She paused to wipe her eyes, and then continued, 'The house and everything is more than anyone could imagine. Everything is so perfect, Thomas. It's just that I wish my ma and Martha could see it. I think of the poverty and sadness back home, and I feel guilty that we have so much.'

Thomas turned her round gently and wiped her eyes with a handkerchief, 'When we get settled, my love, we could bring our families here. They would love it.'

Mary shook her head, 'They would never leave Ireland, never! Sure my ma would hardly leave Kinnego to go to Moville, let alone cross the Atlantic.'

They stood and hugged for a long time, before Thomas said, 'It will only be for a short while. We will be home in no time.'

The following week, Thomas met Lieutenant O'Hare in the town, as promised. He tied his horse outside the hotel and marvelled at the grandeur of all the buildings compared to back home.

As he walked towards the entrance, Lieutenant O'Hare opened the front door and waved to him, 'Thomas, good to see you, my friend. How are you getting settled in?'

Thomas shook his hand as the two of them entered the large restaurant inside the door on the right side, 'I'm good, thanks, Alfred. Mary is very homesick, but I hope she will settle soon.'

'It's a very different life here, Thomas, as many of the immigrants have found out, to their sadness, yet some of them made a great new start,' he laughed.

They sat down at a six seater table and a waiter came to take their drink order. Just then four men came walking in from another part of the hotel. Two of them were dressed in blue army uniforms and were obviously of high rank. The other two were dressed in very expensive suits and wore top hats, which Thomas could hardly stop smiling at.

'May I introduce you to Captain Baird and Colonel Arnold of the Union Army, and Senator King and Senator Mitchell, both of the Republican party.'

Thomas stood up and shook hands with the four, before they joined them at the table.

'Mr Sweeney has just arrived from Ireland with his wife, Mary, and two children,' Lieutenant O'Hare started, 'They own a large estate in Ireland'.

Thomas became uncomfortable as he did not like telling people that he was rich. He preferred to live as the rest of his people.

'Thank you, Alfred, but my wealth means little to me, and came to me through sad circumstances.'

'Did you inherit a business?' asked Senator King.

'No sir, a lot of land in England, which I returned to its rightful owner at a considerable profit.'

'Sounds fascinating, Thomas, chipped in Senator Mitchell, 'you can tell us all one day.'

'So what brings a rich Irishman to our shore?' asked the Colonel, pouring himself some water.

Thomas hesitated, then replied slowly, 'I invent things at home and always wanted to fulfil my late father's dream for me, that I might make things that would change people's lives and livelihoods. It may seem strange, but those opportunities do not exist in Ireland, as yet, as the country is struggling to find its feet after the famine. I have been researching possible opportunities, and have seen, for instance, that your new trains and railways are heavily imported from England. I believe I could change that in time, but that is just one idea.'

The four men looked at him with interest. before the captain spoke, 'It would seem that you have arrived in America at the right time, Thomas. We could use someone as clever as yourself. The Lieutenant here has heard from someone in Ireland who has said that you have made a big difference to the people living in your neighbourhood by introducing new methods of farming.'

'I simply copied what my friend was doing to my land in England,' protested Thomas, sharply, 'It was not my idea, just never tried before in Ireland.'

'Thomas,' began Senator King, 'You may be wondering why the four of us arranged to meet you.'

Thomas was quiet and looked at them with great caution, feeling very uneasy.

'You may not be aware, but it's very likely a war is about to start here,' continued Senator King, taking out a cigar and lighting it, 'We have heard from reliable sources that you are a very clever inventor and a map maker.'

Thomas shifted in his seat and looked at Lieutenant O'Hare.

'You see, Thomas,' proceeded Senator King, in a threatening tone.'If war breaks out, as it surely will, there will only be two types of people. The first will be those on the side of the Union Army, either fighting or helping at home. and those on the Confederate side. who will become our enemy. There will be no in-between, sir, and civilians like yourself will have to take sides, whether they agree with the war or not. It would be wise, sir, as a newcomer, that you familiarise yourself with the situation and decide which side you might favour. If you decide to join us here in the North, then the colonel and I could use someone of your skills.'

There was silence at the table and Thomas felt like walking out. The colonel went on, 'You see, we need a clever man who will think on his feet. We also believe that, as you are a map surveyor, you could be of great help to us.'

'I have just arrived here,' replied Thomas, nervously, 'from a very small country, and have no knowledge of your vast nation, and besides, I have brought my wife and two children here for a new life, to be beside me, not to have me join a war.'

'We reckon you can could be based locally, at our headquarters, where you could look at all our equipment and maps and see how we could improve things. We have just purchased the first automatic rifle in the world and we need a clever person to convince people in authority that it's worth promoting. We also have other new inventions being put to us and we need someone who can test them and recommend changes. We will give you an officer's position, but you will not have to fight if war does break out.'

'This is a big offer, sir, so we will let you have some time to think about it, only let it not be too long as we believe the war will start in the next six months,' said Senator King.

With that the four men rose from the table, thanked Lieutenant O'Hare. and walked out of the hotel. Thomas just sat there staring at the empty glass in front of him. Alfred came back and sat on the chair opposite him, 'Sorry about that, Thomas, I had no idea they were going to spring that on you. The situation is changing very fast.'

Thomas looked at him, with doubt written on his face, 'I did not leave Ireland to get involved in other men's war, and certainly not to join one side against another, in this country.'

Alfred stalled, and then said, wistfully, 'In a war there is always right and wrong, so it's better to find out which side to be on. For me, I believe we should have one United States of America where every man is free, and I think that is worth fighting for.'

Thomas shrugged his shoulders and mounted his horse.

When Thomas arrived at his house he noticed that the carriage was missing. 'Joseph, do you know where the carriage is?' he called.

'I believe Miss Mary went to the city in it, sir, just after you left,' Joseph answered, nervously.

'What?' shouted Thomas, 'why would she do that? She's terrified to set foot in the place.'

'That sounds like the carriage now, sir,' Joseph turned, pointing down the driveway.

Just then the carriage pulled up at the front door and Mary

stepped out. Thomas just stared at her in disbelief and waited for an explanation. Mary looked sad and she spoke softly.

'I went to see the hotel that I worked in after I escaped to thank them for looking after me. It's all boarded up, and a postman told me they both died a few years ago; within weeks of each other. They had no family to take it over. so it went to ruin. They saved my life. I just wanted to thank them.'

'That was generous of you, but not a good idea to go on your own.' Thomas moved close to her and gently moved the hair out of her face, 'I wouldn't want to lose you again.'

'I had Edmond, the driver, with me and we only stopped for a minute. The street seemed very quiet compared to when I escaped.'

They walked hand in hand into the house.

Chapter 8

The next few weeks Thomas tried to keep to himself busy, showing his gardener what he wanted changed in the large expanse of lawn and trees. Mary had tried to question him about his meeting with the four men, but he just shrugged it off. January was ending but no sign of any warmer weather, and there was still an occasional snow shower. Mary was busy every day re-arranging the house to the way she wanted it and trying to get the children into the right school.

The gardener was a black man, called Joseph, aged about fifty. He walked with a slight limp but always had a big smile on his face. Thomas watched him one day from the front door as he wheeled a cart full of manure to spread on the flower beds. 'Joseph,' Thomas called after him, 'It's raining pretty heavily. Take a break in the barn till the shower is over'

'I'm ok master,' replied, Joseph quietly, 'Need to keep working, master.

Thomas went over to him and stood by the side of the cart. 'Now, Joseph,' began Thomas, sternly, 'two things you have to learn today, and you better remember them if you want to keep your job. One: I am not your master, so call me "Thomas", and two: You don't keep working in bad weather. If it's a day like today, find something to do in the barn, and if there is nothing needs doing, then go home.'

Joseph looked at Thomas as if he didn't hear right and went to pick up the cart again. Thomas put his hand on the cart to stop him. 'How much do I pay you, Joseph?' asked Thomas, putting his hand on his shoulder.

'Plenty, master,' replied Joseph, staring at the ground.

'I'll check when I go in, Joseph, and, from today, I will double it. Also, the name's "Thomas". I won't answer you if you call me "master".

Tears appeared in Joseph's eyes. He had no words.

'I never asked you where you live, Joseph.'

Joseph bowed his head to the ground and mumbled a reply. 'In a black ghetto a few miles away, master, along with my daughter.'

'Your daughter?' Thomas asked, sharply, 'You never told me you had a daughter, Joseph. Where is she?'

'Back at home, cleaning our small room,' Joseph added sadly.

'What age is she?'

'Sixteen sir,' Joseph replied nervously.

Thomas just stared at Joseph and could feel himself getting angry inside.

'I will talk more with you later, Joseph. Now go and get out of this rain.' Thomas said, walking back to the house. Mary met him at the door and asked what he was doing. 'We need to extend the servants' quarters out the back into a house for Joseph and his daughter,' Thomas mumbled, as he walked past her.

'Daughter?' Mary exclaimed.

'Will tell you later,' Thomas answered, going into the house.

The next day the sun came out and it was the first day of slightly warmer weather. Mary took the two children in the carriage to the local shops to buy them some new clothes. Thomas opened the back door and found Joseph cleaning out the stables.

'Where are you from, Joseph?' asked Thomas, cheerfully.

'I grew up in the South, Sir,' replied Joseph, slowly.

'Before that, I meant,' Thomas said, reaching for a shovel to help Joseph.

'Please, sir, that is my job,' Joseph said, fearfully.

'I own this house, Joseph, and so I decide what is my job or not, and I am well used to using a shovel. I came from a poor background in Ireland, and I will never forget how to work.'

Joseph was finding this very difficult and could hardly speak, 'I suppose, sir, it's good for us all to do hard work at some point in our life, but if I had your money, I would take a break from it.'

Thomas came and stood in front of Joseph, 'Look, Joseph, the only difference between you and me is that by chance I have become rich. We are both equal in God's sight and if our situation were reversed, I would hope you would treat me the same.'

'My father was a slave, sir, and so was I, till I escaped from the South and found work here. The white man was good to my family and my father never left, even though he had several opportunities. He said he felt safe on the farm and brought three of us up with our own house. We always had food and he gave us Sundays off.'

'Where's your wife now?' Thomas asked slowly.

'She died before we had a chance to leave, sir. She took ill with TB. She was only forty.'

'I'm so sorry. Why then did you leave, Joseph?' Thomas asked gently.

'I watched my daughter grow to accept that life would never change, yet I knew deep inside that there might be an opportunity for us to do more than milk the cows and clean the pig pens. The master was good to us, but I longed to be free to think for myself and give my daughter a better chance in life.'

'Have you found your dream then?' asked Thomas.

'I came north because I heard that there were no slaves, and that masters paid people to work.

I thought I could chose the work that I would do.' He paused, rubbing his hand on his chin. 'I found out that life here is not a lot different, because, unless I were white, I would only get the same type of work as down south. The exception is that here I would be paid, but the difference now is that I have to pay for my lodgings and food, so, while we are free, we're not much better off.'

Thomas paused for a long time. 'There may be a war starting here soon as the president wants to free the slaves down South and create a new nation with one government.'

Joseph looked long at Thomas before replying, 'Not everyone wants to be free, sir, because with freedom comes responsibility and with that a whole new life of decisions.'

'Apart from our colour, we're just the same, though.' Thomas said firmly.

'No, sir, we are not the same. Maybe in the future we will be, but it will take generations before that happens. How we are brought up determines which path we follow. There are many crossroads, where we must chose our own direction and only fate will take us on the right road.'

'I disagree. I believe if we come to know the God who made us, we can then fit into His plan for our life and find contentment, whether we are rich or poor, black or white.'

Joseph looked at Thomas with amazement, 'I have never come across a white man like you, sir. I hope there are many more like you in your country.'

Thomas lifted the spade and threw a pile of manure onto the cart, 'Our land is full of good people, Joseph, but, like here, we have many problems of a different kind. I was wondering, when we go home, would you think about coming with us to live in Ireland?'

Joseph bowed his head again. Once again, words failed him.

'In the meantime, we could do up the second barn that's not being used and very quickly turn it into a good house for you and your daughter.'

Joseph just looked at Thomas with tears in his eyes. 'Why would you do that sir?'

'Because I can, Joseph,' laughed Thomas, walking away, 'We'll start working on that tomorrow, and I want you and your daughter here by next Sunday.'

That evening, Thomas asked Mary to come for a walk along the river that passed the back of their property. They wore heavy warm coats. Although the snow had gone, it was still cold.

'You have been very quiet these last few weeks, Thomas,' Mary started, 'ever since your meeting with those American gentlemen. Is everything alright?'

Thomas walked silently for a while before answering. 'They want me to work for the Union Army, my love. Not as a fighting soldier, but as an adviser.'

Mary kept on walking, looking out at the reflection of the moon on the river. 'What type of adviser? What do you know about war?' she asked eventually.

'They are sure war is about to break out here and they want me to look at all their maps and equipment and see if I can up with any improvements.'

'We did not come all the way from Ireland to become involved in a war,' she paused, 'Who are they going to war with anyway?'

'Their own people. That's why I don't want to become involved.

People here in the North want to free the slaves in the South who work for the big farmers down there.

'Why did they ask you, of all people?' Mary demanded.

'Lieutenant O'Hare obviously told them my life story and they were impressed with the changes I made back home, and also that I have money. I told them that I wasn't interested as I came here to invent machines to help people, not to be involved in killing them.'

'So what is bothering you, then?' Mary asked gently.

'The four men are very important here and they left me with the impression that they were not asking but rather suggesting that, if I were to become successful here in anything, then I would have to help them first.'

Mary went very quiet and walked along the path, with her head down. She took Thomas by the arm, 'Maybe we should go home then. We do not want our children being involved in a war.'

'I have asked Joseph and his daughter to come and live on our land, by the way.', Thomas sighed.

Mary stopped and looked at him in disbelief. They came to the end of the riverside path and turned to go home. It was now very dark.

Two weeks later

Thomas and Mary and the children alighted from the carriage at their front door. It was Sunday and they had just been to the local church, a mile away. The church was white with a small spire and was set on the top of a small hill. There were about fifty locals there and lots of children for Michael and Colleen to make friends with. The folks were extremely kind to Thomas and Mary and made them feel at home with gifts of local food and fruit. They were about to go inside, when a carriage pulled into their driveway and stopped beside them.

Colonel Arnold stepped down from the carriage dressed in his full Union Army uniform.

'Good day to you, sir,' he said, shaking Thomas by the hand, 'This must be your wonderful family.'

Mary just stared at him and pulled the children to her side.

'What can I do for you today, Colonel?' asked Thomas.

The colonel moved to one side and patted one of the horses. 'Sadly, Thomas, it looks like we are about to declare war on the South. We have tried all routes of negotiation but it seems that there is too big a gap between us. it's not what we want, but if we are to have a country with one government and with freedom for all, then it looks like it will have to be won the hard way.'

'I find it hard to believe, Colonel, that Americans are going to kill each other for an ideal, that seems to be less clear cut, the more I talk to people from both sides.'

The colonel seemed annoyed at Thomas, but appealed to him, 'Well, that's the way it's, sir, and you will have to decide now which side you and your family are on. If you are not with us it will be very hard for us to protect your property, should the Southern Army get this far.'

Thomas turned to Mary, 'Take the family inside please, Mary. I need to talk to the Colonel.'

Mary hesitated, then turned with anger in her eyes and pulled Michael and Colleen in the front door and banged it shut.

'What do you want?' Thomas asked, sharply.

'As we said, Thomas, it's now very urgent that we check our maps before we send thousands of our young men to battle in an area that we are not sure about. Thomas stood staring at the ground, saying nothing for a long time. 'If I do this, and I mean "if", can you guarantee the safety of my family and house while I'm away?' Thomas challenged the colonel.

'Absolutely, sir. If war breaks out, then I will personally make sure that there will be a unit of my men who will guard this area day and night, and if the Southerners ever get this far, then we will move them to safety. Anyway, you'll be based near here.'

'When would I need to start, Colonel?' asked Thomas, looking troubled.

'Tomorrow sir,' replied the colonel, climbing into his coach. 'I can arrange all your transport for you for the first week till you find your way.'

'I will go and talk to Mary now,' Thomas said, turning to the front door.

'I must have your decision, now. I cannot wait another hour.'

Thomas turned and glared at him, and paused for a minute, 'Right, then, I will do it.'

The carriage moved off with the colonel shouting. 'Be ready at dawn. I will send a uniform with the carriage. Oh...and we've decided to make you a captain!'

Thomas and Mary barely spoke for the next few hours, till dinner time, when he decided to break the news to the children. 'This will only be for a short time, and then I will have access to very powerful men who can help me start my business.'

Michael, who was now coming fourteen, was a thinker, and was not easily convinced of his father's plan.

'It sounds like a trap, Da,' he said, standing up from the kitchen table. 'Why would they want you in uniform if you are just going to advise them on maps?'

Thomas didn't answer as he knew his son was not going to be easily fooled.

Colleen joined in, which surprised Thomas, as she was normally very quiet. 'Will you have to go away, Da? It sounds very strange.'

Thomas came around the table and gave her a big hug, 'I'll not be going anywhere, Colleen, my love. I'll be working a very short distance away from here.'

Thomas could sense that he was not convincing any of his family, so he excused himself and went upstairs to his room.

Chapter 9

Thomas was very quiet over breakfast, and Mary had warned the children not to ask questions. He could hardly eat the eggs and toast, and pushed aside his coffee. Mary walked around the kitchen trying to hide her tears – and her fear. Thomas got up and lifted his coat from the back of the chair. 'I promise this will be only a short while,' he choked out, as he put his arms around Michael and Colleen, 'Then I will be back to start my business and forget about talk of war. Now you two, I need you to look after your ma, and be extra good for her, and I will be home every evening.'

There was silence from everyone, and Thomas began to feel he was making a big mistake. He turned to Mary, as he put on his coat, 'I don't know how to get out of this, Mary. These are very powerful men and. if I refuse, we may as well get the next ship back to Ireland.'

'That would be far better, Thomas. This is so out of character for you. It's like a bad dream – or worse.'

Mary turned and started washing dishes in the sink to hide her tears. Thomas walked out the door without looking back.

There was an army carriage waiting at the door with two soldiers waiting for him.

'Good morning, sir,' said the sergeant, 'We need to leave now. There's a uniform for you on the seat.'

Thomas nodded as he climbed into the coach. The sergeant and the other soldier sat outside and left Thomas to sit in the coach on his own.

2 months later - 12th April 1861

Thomas said goodbye to Mary and the children at the front door and was about to mount his horse to go to work when a soldier came galloping up their drive and pulled his horse to a sudden stop. 'Captain,' he started, out of breath, 'I have been sent to fetch you, and to inform you that war has been declared with the Confederates. All soldiers are being summoned to base for instructions.'

Thomas stared at the soldier for a few minutes and then replied slowly, 'I am not a regular soldier. I am a volunteer map maker.'

'I am not aware of what you do, Captain, I'm just following orders,' he said, as he turned his horse and galloped away.

Thomas looked at Mary who was now sheltering the children. 'It will be all right, darling.' I have been promised that I will never have to fight. I will go now and see what they want, but will be back at the usual time.' Thomas turned and hugged Mary and the children. 'The war will be fought a long way from here. We will all be safe.'

Thomas mounted his horse and turned and rode down the drive. 'An Irish stew would be grand tonight, my love. See you all later.'

'Why is da going to war, ma?' asked Michael, as he stepped out to watch his father's horse gallop down the lane. 'He hates violence of any kind and he said he would never fight here in America.'

'I know, son,' Mary said sadly, 'If he says he will not fight, then I believe him, I'm sure he has been called in for a good reason.'

'What exactly is war?' asked Colleen, sitting down on the front step.

'War is when people do not get on, my love, and they start shooting guns at each other.'

'They don't shoot guns at each other in Ireland, ma, even when they don't get on.'

'I know, Colleen, but we're not at home now, my love,' Mary said softly.

'When will we go home again? I miss the sea and my swing in the tree.'

Mary came and hugged Colleen, 'Very soon, my love, very soon.'

Thomas arrived at the Union Army headquarters and tied his horse beside the many other horses by the front door. As he entered the door, Colonel Arnold was standing addressing a group of officers in the large front hall. Thomas could see paintings of officers and battles covering most of the walls. There was a high ceiling with a glass roof; something Thomas had never seen before. He expected to see more military ware in the room and was quite surprised at the opulence. He was happy to see a large table at the far end spread with food for the men. Thomas stood quietly behind the colonel till he finished addressing the officers. He turned and realised Thomas had joined them. 'Gentlemen,' he started in a louder voice, 'May I introduce Captain Sweeney from Ireland. He is here at my invitation and is going to help us with technical planning. He has no soldier training or background but I want him to be treated as one of our own as I believe his technical skills may save many lives. Come in, Captain, and help yourself to some breakfast.'

Thomas felt very awkward, wanting to leave straight away, till one of the sergeants came up and introduced himself. He escorted Thomas to the food table.

'You will soon find your way about, Captain. Till then, come and learn how to eat,' he laughed.

'I'm Sergeant Wilson, by the way, and my father was Irish.'

Soon all the officers were helping themselves to the breakfast and making very loud conversation.

Colonel Arnold entered the room as the men were finishing breakfast and came and sat opposite Thomas with a bundle of maps in his arm. The soldiers on his right got up to give him room, as Thomas looked on with concern. The colonel spread the maps out in front of Thomas.

'Take a look at these, Captain, and tell me what you think?' Colonel Arnold said, reaching for a cigar.

Thomas turned the maps around and sat there looking at them quietly. He read them carefully knowing he was about to be asked a lot of questions. He moved nervously in his chair as he realised that the colonel may not be pleased with his reaction.

'Not good, Captain,' murmured the colonel, 'your silence tells me a lot.'

Thomas took a deep breath, 'I presume, sir, that these maps were produced some time ago.'

Colonel Arnold just nodded.

'I find it hard to believe that these are professional maps, sir. I can see that there are areas here that have not been properly surveyed, as distances seem to suddenly change.'

'Exactly, Captain,' replied Arnold, stubbing out his cigar 'Our general, McDowell, is about to send thirty-five thousand troops to Virginia and we don't even know the territory that we are sending them to, even though it's only a hundred miles away. There is talk of using the railways to transport the men, but that would leave us open to sabotage by the Greycoats, so he may march them there using maps that are not accurate'

Thomas shifted in his seat uncomfortably for he knew what was coming next.

'We need your skills, son,' insisted the colonel, as he folded up the maps. 'We can't risk sending men to fight on our orders, when we have not got the right information in front of us.'

'I don't see how I can help, Colonel,' began Thomas slowly, 'It would take a long time to survey this area properly, and I gather that you don't have time.'

'We don't need the whole area surveyed, Captain,' Colonel Arnold grunted, as he unfolded one of the maps again and pointed at one place on the page. 'This is Shenandoah valley. It's the place where we believe we can win the first battle and, with any luck, the last. We feel we can take on the Greycoats and thrash them so that the war can be over in a month. or maybe two. So you see, it's vital that we have an up-to-date detailed map of the area.'

'The Confederates must know that area well, Colonel, and if war has been declared, then it would be impossible for anyone to survey that area,' Thomas replied sternly.

'Difficult, but not impossible for a clever Irish man, like yourself. You would be there as a private contractor out of uniform and we could arrange for an alibi from our map making company. You would be in and out of the area in a few days, before any soldiers arrive there.'

Thomas rose from the table, hiding his anger. 'Colonel, may I suggest that you use an American surveyor, who at least knows the area, as I would have to ask local people for information.'

'We were told that you were one of the best map surveyors in your country, and we need someone with that type of skill to do this right, as lives will depend on it. I can not order you to do this, as you are a volunteer, and you can walk away from the army at any time, but my commanders have told me to ask you if you will do this for us.' Arnold folded up the map again and turned to walk away, 'I need an answer by tonight. as you would have to leave tomorrow.'

Thomas watched him walk out the door, before he shrugged his shoulders and left by the door he had come in. He was so annoyed that he got on his horse and rode home.

Mary was in the garden talking to Joseph when Thomas galloped up the driveway and jumped off his horse at the front door.

'Thomas,' Mary called, 'Why are you home so early?'

Thomas turned in anger and walked through the front door.

'Doesn't look so good, ma'am' Joseph said quietly.

'No it doesn't, Joseph. I'd better go and see what is wrong. Thank you for showing me the flower bed arrangement. it's perfect.' With that, she walked quickly towards the house.

Mary found Thomas in the kitchen staring at a painting of his family that hung on the wall overlooking the table. She went up behind him and put her arm around his waist, but said nothing.

'They want me to go to the war zone, Mary, and spy out the land for a big battle. They say I will be safe in ordinary clothes and I can pretend to be working for a surveying company.'

Mary was still quiet and hugged him harder.

'I did not come all the way from Ireland to do this, let alone spy for them. The Colonel told me that, as a volunteer, I could leave the army, but I know that the engineering projects I have been working on for them would stop. I have designed ways to improve their new automatic guns and at the end of the war, I know I could set up a company that would serve the government and then go on to bigger private projects.' Thomas paused and turned to Mary, 'I have to decide if it's worth risking my life for my dream and, right now, I don't think it's.'

'You always make the right decision, and I will stand by you, no matter what you decide,' Mary said, putting her arms around his neck.

'They want me to decide now, as I would have to leave in the morning,' Thomas said sadly.

They stood hugging each other in silence for a long time.

Chapter 10

Thomas sat in the train, looking out the window at the countryside rolling by. Sometimes great black clouds from the noisy steam engine would block out the blue sky. He was sitting on his own, as the rest of the carriage was empty. No one wanted to travel South today as no one knew where the enemy would be. He longed to be back home by the sea in Donegal and wondered what had ever possessed him to bring his family to America. He could hear the waves crashing on the beach in Kinnego Bay and could smell the crystal clear water as it broke on the rocks. Just then, a soldier entered the carriage, carrying a piece of paper.

'Excuse me, Captain,' he started quietly. 'My apologies for disturbing you, sir, but I was given this letter to hand to you before our last stop in North Virginia, which is coming up shortly.'

He handed Thomas the paper, which opened and read the brief instructions. 'Thank you, corporal, how long have you been in the army?'

'One year, sir. I joined when I turned sixteen,' the young soldier replied nervously.

'Why did you join the army?' asked Thomas bluntly, 'You are only a boy.'

'My father said it was a good job in these times and I liked the idea of excitement.'

Thomas looked him in the eye for some time until the young soldier dropped his gaze to the floor. 'You are too young to die, son,' he continued softly. 'If they send you to the front line to fight, then don't try and be a hero. Stay back from the line as far as you can so that some day you can become a living hero to your own son which, believe me, is far better.'

The young corporal had never heard anyone speak like this before and became nervous. 'Thank you for your advice, Captain. I hope we will meet again one day.' With that, he was gone.

The train started to slow down, so Thomas lifted his equipment and headed for the door.

The train stopped at a very deserted looking station and, as Thomas stepped down from the train, all he could see through the smoke and steam was a large water tank with a wind wheel beside it. Thomas was the only person who got off the train and, a few seconds later, it pulled out of the station, leaving him standing in the cold air looking out at endless dust fields. The dirt track ran in both directions from the station, and suddenly Thomas could see three horses approaching from the left. He suddenly felt very alone and wondered what he was doing when two soldiers, with a third horse behind them, pulled up at the front of the station.

'Howdy!' the first soldier called, sliding off his horse. 'You must be the mystery man we have been ordered to meet. We have a horse for you.' He pulled the spare horse around to give Thomas the reins.

'Where is this place?' asked Thomas.

'We are very close to the Shenandoah Valley, just down that way,' answered the first soldier pointing south.

'You know where you're going?' the second soldier asked.

'Nope,' replied Thomas, shrugging his shoulders, 'but I have maps of sorts.'

'Maps won't do you any good out here, sir,' the first soldier said, climbing back on his horse. 'I reckon it's only twenty miles till ya come across the Greycoats down that way, so, if I were you, I would make sure you stay this side of the river.'

'Thank you, soldier,' replied Thomas, as he packed his equipment into the side saddles on either side of his new brown horse.

With that the soldiers were off at a gallop, leaving a great cloud of dust as they vanished down the track.

Thomas headed south with a steep mountain range to his right and a large winding river to his left. He had only gone a few miles when the river started to disappear behind trees and the path he was following started to dip down towards a valley. He pulled the horse to a stop and unfolded one of his maps. Suddenly he heard the whine of a bullet passing very close to his head and the horse jumped as a gunshot sound followed from the trees. Thomas remembered being shot at back in England and it didn't take him long to react. Diving off his horse and crouching down, he tried to see where the shot had come from. Just then six Confederate soldiers emerged from the trees pointing their guns at him and shouting at him to stay still. Thomas heart was pounding in his chest and he could hardly speak, as the men approached him.

The soldier with stripes on his uniform shouted to him. 'Put your gun down, Yankee.'

'I don't have a gun,' replied Thomas, nervously, 'This is a map.'

The soldiers surrounded him, taking his horse by the reins and pulling it away from him.

The sergeant came up close still pointing his revolver at him. 'What are you doing here Yankee?' he snapped.

'I am not a Yankee, sir,' replied Thomas, in a broken voice. 'I'm from Ireland and I'm working for a map-making company in New York.'

'If you are making a map during war, then you are a Yankee spy,' snapped the sergeant.

'No, sir, I have all my equipment with me and have just got off the train back there a few miles.'

The sergeant came and opened his saddle bags and pulled out some of his survey poles before shoving them back in again. 'You will have to come with us. Our army is the other side of the river and we're expecting the Yankee army to come down this way. If you stay here, you will be in the middle of a war, and no one is going to ask you what side you are on. Give the man his horse. You are bleeding.' He turned to one of the soldiers, 'Get his leg seen to. Then bring him back to camp.'

Thomas was sick in his stomach as he climbed back onto his horse and started to follow the sergeant back towards the trees with one soldier behind him. Although his leg was bleeding he felt no pain and was relieved that it must only be a graze.

They came to a clearing and Thomas was shocked to see that the soldiers had made a wooden bridge stretching right across the wide river. This will be some surprise to the Union soldiers he thought, as he knew they thought the Confederates would be unable to cross the fast flowing river. At the far end of the river, they turned south again and, within a mile, came to a huge flat expanse of land with thousands of soldiers camped on it. The sergeant led Thomas to a tent in the middle of the camp that had a flag pole beside it and armed soldiers standing at each side of it.

'Wait there, Irishman,' the sergeant said, as he disappeared into the tent. Thomas looked all around him and realised that when his Union soldiers came into the valley, they were going to get some shock and would probably be defeated by such a well-equipped army. He had been misinformed and convinced that they were only a bunch of rebels!

The sergeant re-appeared from the tent followed by a senior officer with stripes on his uniform.

'This is General Beauregard,' said the sergeant, proudly, 'He is commanding officer of our army, and this is the Irishman we found wandering through the valley.'

Thomas climbed down off his horse and stood in front of the general.

'And what brings an Irishman all the way here, with a war on?'

'My company in New York, whom I have only started working for, sent me to update maps of this entire region,' replied Thomas.

'What is the name of your company, son?' asked the general.

'The Hudson Bay Geographical Company, sir; the surveying department.'

'Why should I not have you shot for spying? Your company must be working for the Yankees.'

'I arrived from Ireland, sir, with my family, to start a business and make a new life. I have no interest in American politics or war. We are only here since January. Had I known that your country was at war, I would have stayed at home! I wish to return to Ireland immediately after I arrive back in New York.'

The general stared at Thomas for a long time then laughed, 'If you ever see New York again, son. Sergeant get the man some food and lodging. He looks like he needs it.' He patted Thomas on the shoulder and walked back to his tent. 'Were there Union soldiers on your journey here, Irishman?' he turned and asked Thomas.

'The train was empty, sir.'

The general gave a grunt and disappeared into his tent.

'You are not a prisoner, Irish, but you will have to stay with us now just in case you carry any information back to the Bluecoats,' the sergeant said, as he motioned for Thomas to follow him.

Thomas was surprised at how comfortable his tent was and the food he was brought was like a home-cooked dinner. He had his own bed and a chair with a wash basin and towel and a small chest to put his things in. These people seem very nice he thought and somehow, he felt more at home with them than with the folks back in New York. He had just finished his meal that someone had brought him, when a soldier came into his tent.

'Well, Paddy, what's your name?' the soldier asked, with a Mayo accent.

Thomas smiled and was delighted to hear an Irish accent, 'Thomas Sweeney from Donegal,' he said. 'And you are?'

'Private Timothy O'Brien at your service, Sweeney,' he said, sitting down on the chair, 'What on earth are you doing here, lad?'

'Making maps, Timothy.'

'Ah, sure you are, Sweeney, pull the other one!' O'Brien laughed.

Thomas sat on the bed facing him, 'No, I am, seriously.'

'Maps for the Yanks, so they can find their way down South here, as most of them have never been outside New York.'

Thomas looked at the ground, and stared for a long time. 'I don't know why all the Americans want to kill each one another when all I want to do is live in peace with my family.'

Timothy lit a pipe and stared at Thomas, 'Where's your family, Sweeney?'

'Back in my house, just outside New York.'

'How many?'

'My wife and two children,' replied Thomas, with sadness in his voice.

'You might not see them for a while as they won't let you leave here till the war is over, and that might be a few months.'

'I wish I had kept them in Ireland, Timothy. What is this stupid war all about anyway?'

'Freedom, Thomas! The Yankees want to control all the Southern states as well as their own.'

Timothy stood up, 'There are a lot of Irish going to fight in this war, but they will fight for the side which gives them the best deal, not for their cause.'

'I have to get home to my family, Timothy, I don't want to fight.' Thomas said, standing up in a panic, 'I shouldn't be here.'

Timothy stood up, and went to the door of the tent, saying, 'Let me see what I can do, lad?' With that, he was gone.

Chapter 11

The next morning, Thomas was summoned to the general's tent. As Thomas entered, he was surprised to see so many senior officers standing in a circle at the far end along with the general.

They were looking at a large map spread on the floor. The general looked up when Thomas was shown in by a soldier.

'Irishman, come in,' he called, motioning to the others to make space for him to join the circle.

'If you are a map maker, what do you make of this?'

Thomas looked down at a very crude map of their present area. 'This is old,' was his first response, aware that his life might depend on every word he said. There was silence for a while. Thomas continued, 'As far as I can tell, this is very inaccurate, gentlemen.' He paused, and knelt down to point out part of the map. 'I have just come through this part, and the river is not as close to the mountains as this map shows. There's a huge open valley here, perhaps five to six miles across, with no shelter.'

'Where did you come from?' asked one of the senior officers.

'The last train stop, here,' pointed Thomas.

'Did you see soldiers while you were on the train?' asked another officer.

'No, sir,' replied Thomas, standing up 'There were a couple of young soldiers acting as guards, but that was it.'

'This changes everything, men,' stated the general. 'If the Yankees are using the same bad map as this then they won't be expecting us to attack them in the Shenandoah valley, so that is where we will plan our next step.'

The map was rolled up and the officers started moving into pairs to have private talks.

'What are we going to do with you, Irishman?' the general motioned to Thomas to sit opposite him at a small table. 'Would you join our army and fight against out intruders.'

Thomas stared straight at the general and said quietly, 'I came to this land, sir, to fulfil a life-long dream of inventing new ways of helping people, to make life easier – not killing them, sir. I am a man of peace with no idea of the politics of this country and all I want to do is to take my family back to Ireland.'

'What is your name, Irish?' asked the general, kindly.

'Thomas, sir. Thomas Sweeney from Donegal.'

The general took out a pipe and looked closely at Thomas. 'I believe you son, but I can not let you go as you might run into the Bluecoats and give them information about our army.'

'You have treated me very well, general, and I can see that I would be happier living with your people than the people I have met in New York, but I understand it would be difficult for you to trust me, but for one thing.'

The general put his pipe down and peered at Thomas, 'And what would that be?'

'I noticed, on the way to your tent, that you have a large pile of the new Winchester rifles sitting unused.'

'You're very observant, Irish.' The general lit his pipe.

'The Union soldiers are planning to use them, only they are nervous of change at this late stage.' Thomas moved nervously.

'And how do you know this?' The general asked sharply.

'They asked me to train them,' Thomas answered, nervously.

Thomas was taking a huge risk, telling him this, but he felt that he could trust this man more than any of the Union soldiers he had met. The general just stared at Thomas for a long time.

'And why are you risking your life telling me this now?' He blew smoke from his pipe directly towards Thomas.

'If you see me safe home, general, then I will show you how the new rifles work and try and convince your men that they will win the war if they use them.'

The general stood up and came round to Thomas. 'Come and show me, Irish.' He motioned

Thomas to follow him out of the tent.

Thomas picked up one of the rifles and asked a soldier beside him to fetch some ammunition. The soldier guarding the general, became very uneasy, but the general told him to relax. The soldier handed the box of ammunition to Thomas, who proceeded to load the rifle.

'If this is one of your current rifles, and suppose I fire one shot at a target, then it will take me at least ten seconds to reload the rifle and fire again. By this time I may be dead. However, if I use this new rifle, this is what I can do.' Thomas aimed the new rifle at a water barrel one hundred yards away and shot off the magazine in a few seconds, leaving the water barrel with dozens of holes in it. Soldiers standing nearby jumped and ran to the general, thinking there was an attack.

'It's ok, men,' shouted the general, 'It's a demonstration of how we can win this war.' He turned to Thomas. 'None of my men wanted to swap their old rifles for these as they're averse to change, but hopefully, they will see now just how fast these guns really are.'

Thomas took the rifle and showed the firing catch to the general. 'There is a slight flaw in the design, General. I did not show the

Bluecoats this as they were too arrogant to listen to me. You see the safety catch here? If it's screwed off and put on the other way around it can be flicked off very quickly and will avoid the risk of jamming the trigger as it swings away from the pin.'

'I am impressed, Irish. What did you say your name was?'

'Thomas, sir,'replied Thomas quietly.

'It will be hard to get you back to New York, Thomas, but I think you've earned your way. Give me a few days to think of a plan.'

The general walked away and the other soldiers stood and stared at Thomas.

Thomas had just finished a hearty dinner that evening, when Timothy came into his tent.

'Well Thomas Sweeney, you have made some impression on the big brass, and what a noise you have made all afternoon!'

'I introduced them to the new automatic rifle that was sitting unused.'

'It's amazing! The men have been playing with them all afternoon. It's some weapon!'

'Unfortunately it will kill a lot more people than your old one, Timothy.' Thomas looked sad.

'That is true, Thomas, but it may save life in the end as it will shorten the war.'

Thomas cleared his plate away. 'War solves nothing, and some day everyone will have to sit down and talk, so why not talk now and save thousands of lives?'

'I said before, Thomas, talking does not produce power; only the gun will do that,' Timothy said, as he lit a cigarette.

'I believe words can be more powerful than the gun. It's how they are used that determines life or death.'

'The general asked me to help you get back up north.' Timothy said, smiling. 'It seems they are going to trust you not to tell the Bluecoats about our army.'

'What army?' smiled Thomas.

'I will let you get some sleep, lad,' Timothy said, as he headed out the tent door. 'See you in the morning.'

Thomas woke the next morning to the sound of a bugle. He peered out the tent door and all he could see were soldiers running in all directions, some pulling their uniform on as they ran. Timothy appeared suddenly and shouted at Thomas, 'Get dressed quickly, Thomas! The enemy has been spotted a few miles away!'

Thomas dressed slowly, as he had no intention of getting involved in the battle that might be about to start. Timothy appeared again at the tent door. 'We're going to have our first battle, Thomas! The Bluecoats are going to march straight into the valley, not knowing we will have them cornered like sheep, only I'm not going to see it, damn it!'

'Why not?' asked Thomas, as he finished pulling on his jacket.

'Because I have been given orders to escort you east of the valley, then north, away from the Union army, so that you can get home to your family.'

Thomas couldn't answer. He was shocked, that the general would actually keep his word. He was about to gather up his clothes, when Timothy told him that they would have to make the journey on foot, as, going by horse, the Bluecoats would see them. Thomas went back into the tent and packed a few personal things into a small bag and Timothy gave him a bag of supplies that would last a week. Thomas and Timothy were about to set off when the general came up behind them. 'I wish you well Irish,' he shouted, above the noise. 'We owe you a lot, and when we win this awful war, your name will be mentioned, son. Go home to Ireland and enjoy your life in peace.'

With that, he turned and walked fast back towards his tent.

Thomas and Timothy walked towards a line of trees, and it wasn't long before the noise of the camp became faint.

'I am to take you as far north as the railway station, Thomas, and then you are on your own,' Timothy said, sounding quite annoyed. 'You must be a very special person that our general would let you go, when the rest of us are off to fight for our land.'

'That's the difference, Timothy,' Thomas replied, stopping and looking him in the eye. 'This is your land, it's not mine.'

'It's not mine either, but they are paying me good money to keep it for them.'

Thomas shrugged his shoulders and turned, walking off towards the forest.

Chapter 12

Mary was standing by the sink, looking out the kitchen window which overlooked the front garden. It was hard to believe that it was a month, to this day, since Thomas set off on his journey down south. There was no word from him, even though he had promised to keep in touch. She was growing sick with worry, especially now she knew that huge numbers of Union troops had been sent on the next train on which Thomas had left. She was barely able to concentrate on her chores every day as she was constantly quietly praying that God would take care of Thomas and bring him home. They had always prayed together before making major decisions in life. and so she was very concerned that Thomas had made the decision to go and spy for the army without her consent.' Very unlike Thomas,' she said to herself.

Suddenly Michael and Colleen came trudging up the driveway, having been dropped by the coach at the front gate. Mary dried her hands and ran to meet them at the door.

'Hello, my loves. How was school today?' she laughed, even though she was sad inside.

'A bit strange today,' Colleen answered, as she hugged her mother. 'A soldier came to school to tell us about the war that is starting.'

'Why would they do that now, my love?' encouraged Mary. 'Sure it's a long way away from here, and will never affect us.'

'Did da write yet, Ma?' Colleen asked, sadly.

'Not yet, but I am sure he will. Mary stood up to go into the house as Michael slammed the front door behind him.

Mary looked alarmed and took Colleen's hand to walk inside. 'Michael!' she called as they closed the front door behind them. There was silence, and Mary could hear a noise from his bedroom upstairs.

'Help yourself to some soda bread, Colleen, while I go and see what is wrong with your brother,' Mary said gently, as she climbed the stairs. She opened Michael's room and found him staring out the window. 'What's wrong with my big son, today?' she asked in a calm voice. Michael didn't reply, but just kept staring out the window. Mary went to him and put her arm around his shoulder.

'I want to join the army, Ma,' Michael said suddenly. 'I want to follow da and join the fight for freedom.'

Mary was utterly shocked, but tried to make light of Michael's statement. She knew she had to be careful with every word she would say over the next few minutes.

'Who on earth put that idea in your head?'

'A soldier came to our school today to tell us all about the war that's starting and how, once we are sixteen, we could enlist to defend our country against the South,' Michael said sharply.

'Look at me, Michael,' Mary said gently as she turned him round to face her. 'First thing, son, this is not our land; nor is it our fight. Secondly, you are only just turned fourteen and the war will probably be over by the time you're sixteen. Thirdly, your da did not go off to fight or spy. He went south to make maps, which was his old trade.'

'I can't stay here every day, Ma, knowing that da might need help. I need to join up now.'

Mary gave him a big hug.'Come and have some soda bread, son. We will talk about this later.'

Mary tried to hide her fear and sadness, as they ate dinner later that evening. Michael, even though he was fourteen, looked like he was eighteen and was very mature and strong like his father. Mary helped them with their homework, which consisted of stories of American history. They were all unusually quiet going to bed and Mary prayed with them both before saying goodnight.

Summer had started early, and the garden was teaming with colour in the bright sunshine as all the flowers and bushes that they had planted together began to bud and flower. Michael and Colleen had gone to school after breakfast and Mary was about to take a trip to the village when Joseph, the gardener, walked past the front door, 'Morning, Ma'am. 'Tis a fine day today. Looks like winter has gone for another year.'

'Morning, Joseph,' Mary replied, very glad to see him. 'Have you heard any news about the war yet?'

'Because of my colour, Ma'am, not many people would confide in me, but I have heard from folks down the road that the first battle of the war has started in Shenandoah Valley and that they're sending a lot of new recruits on the train every day.' Joseph dropped his eyes to the ground. 'I hope master is not near those parts, Ma'am.'

'Me too, Joseph, me too,' Mary sighed.

'I am sure Master will be fine now, Ma'am. He's a very bright man and he will know how to look after himself.'

'Where's your daughter Joseph?' Mary asked, concerned.

'She is working round the back, Ma'am.'

'We need to find a school for her, Joseph. At sixteen, she needs to be trained to do a proper job.'

'She happy, Ma'am,' Joseph smiled.

'We will talk later, Joseph. What's her name again?'

'Charity, Ma'am.'

'Nice name, Joseph. I'll be back soon,' she said, as she climbed into the coach and asked the driver to take her to the shops.

In the village, she got talking to some of the new friends she had made, and even had lunch with a few of them, before asking the driver to take her home. She hadn't meant to stay so long, and was getting back at the same time as Michael and Colleen were due home. The coach pulled up to the front door, just as Colleen came walking up the drive way.

'Where's Michael?' Mary shouted to Colleen

'Don't know, Ma,' answered Colleen with a worried voice, 'He wasn't in school all day.'

'What do you mean, he wasn't in school?' she yelled as she ran to the side of the house, before asking Joseph to look after Colleen. She must find Michael!

Mary asked the coach driver to take her the two miles to the school, and got there as the headmistress was just closing up the school. She didn't wait for the coach to stop properly before jumping off quickly.

'Have you seen Michael Sweeney, Miss?' she called frantically.

'No Ma'am,' the headmistress replied. 'I thought you would know where he is as he didn't come to school today.'

Mary knew in her heart where he was, but could not bring herself to believe it. She jumped back into the coach and told the driver to race to the nearest army barracks, six miles away.

As the driver sped into the army compound, Mary jumped out of the coach and ran towards the front door. A sergeant, who was coming out, stopped her. 'Easy, Ma'am! Where are you going in such a rush?'

'I'm looking for my son, sir; a young boy who may have come here on his own to join the army,' Mary said, almost crying.

'We have hundreds of young boys coming here, Miss, to join up. He may be around the back, at the recruitment centre,' the sergeant said kindly, sensing Mary's distress. 'Let me take you there, as you could get lost in here.'

The sergeant escorted Mary around the right side of the building and took her on a walk that was nearly a quarter of a mile to a small wooden cabin used for signing up new recruits. 'Let me enquire for you, ma'am.' The soldier stopped her from entering. 'It can be very noisy in there right now. What is your son's name?'

'Michael Sweeney, sir,' replied Mary. 'He's only fourteen.'

'I doubt if he was here, Ma'am,' the sergeant said cautiously, 'They won't sign up anyone under sixteen.'

'Just check please,' Mary pleaded. The sergeant went into the hut, as Mary sat on bench in the sun.

The sergeant came out after twenty minutes with a Lieutenant, both looking very serious.

'Good evening, Mrs Sweeney. My name is Lieutenant Jameson. I am one of the recruitment officers. I believe you are looking for your son, Michael.'

'I am, Sir. He is only a young boy and I think he may have come here this morning, instead of going to school.'

'I have looked at our list and, sure enough, his name is on it, but he told us he was seventeen and he certainly looks very much the age he gave us.'

'Where is he, Sir? I want to take him home.'

The sergeant will take you to the uniform store, Ma'am, where, hopefully, he will still be, as the lads who joined up haven't been shipped out on the train yet.'

The sergeant led Mary to a long building across a big green square, where new recruits were already standing chatting to each other while waiting for their orders. The sergeant suggested that Mary should wait, to avoid embarrassing Michael, as he went in to find him.

Five minutes later he emerged with Michael, looking very guilty, and the sergeant handed him over to Mary. Michael was holding his new uniform in his arm, which the sergeant gently removed from him. 'Come back in two years, son. It will be waiting for you.'

Mary said nothing, but the two of them walked back to the coach.

The first night for Thomas and Timothy was cold and scary. They didn't want to light a fire in the forest in case there were stray Union soldiers who had somehow made it across to their side of the river. They chatted about Ireland, the war and what new life in America might look like once things returned to normal. Thomas was tired, and suggested that they get to sleep early. He hoped he was not going to have to walk a hundred miles back to New York.

Thomas woke early the next morning to find Timothy missing from his side. He jumped up and thought about calling for him but decided to go and look for him instead. He had gone about two hundred yards when he heard the sound of gunfire and cannons in the distance. Timothy appeared from behind a mound that led down towards the river.

'I need to go, Thomas,' he announced, as he walked back to get his rifle and gear.

'Go where, Timothy?' asked Thomas, alarmed.

'The battle has started and I need to go and join my men.' He picked up his rifle and slung it on his shoulder. 'I was told to take you north to the railway station and then come back. That's impossible now, as the Yankees have made it to the valley. I have to go and fight with my men, Thomas.'

Thomas just stared at him and realised that saying anything would be pointless, so he bade him farewell, 'Don't waste your life on another man's war, Timothy. Promise me you will take great care, so that one day we may meet again.'

Timothy looked at him then shrugged his shoulders. 'Maybe, lad. Do you know where you're going?'

'No, but I'm sure I'll find my way eventually,' replied Thomas sadly.

'Keep to this side of the river for about ten miles, till you come to a railway bridge. Then follow the tracks to the first station. You never know, the trains might still be running.' With that, he was gone. He didn't even wave goodbye.

Thomas gathered up all his gear and started walking north. The forest started to thin out as the high ground got closer on his right side. There was no path, so his progress was slow. He came to a stream that was a yard wide, flowing into the river, and he had to jump across it. The sun was getting warmer, and he was enjoying the scenery all around him, although, with every mile he travelled, the noise of the battle on the other side of the river became louder.

He was aware that he was now walking in open ground, but was hoping that all the soldiers on the far side of the river would be too busy in battle to notice a man walking with no uniform. A path appeared in front of him, and it seemed to lead up a steep hill, so he decided that was the only way he could keep heading north. He was near the top of the hill when he heard voices, and so he crouched down to look over a grass mound. He was shocked to see about twenty well-dressed men and women having a picnic, overlooking the battle that was going on below.

Several men, donned in top hats and dinner suits, were drinking champagne from real glasses. After ten minutes, he decided that it might be safe to go and talk to them.

'Good day,' Thomas ventured, coming up behind them.

Two of the gentlemen turned sharply, but when they saw Thomas was a civilian, they replied.

'Coming to join the party, Sir?' the tallest man laughed.

Thomas kept walking towards them and said nothing, being utterly shocked that anyone would be having a party overlooking a battle, where men were dying.

'Great battle,' the smaller man said, holding out a glass to Thomas.

Thomas declined, and turned to see what they were watching. In the centre of the valley were thousands of Union soldiers, some on horse back and some with horses pulling heavy guns. What shocked Thomas was that the Confederates had them surrounded and were mowing them down with automatic weapons. Thomas felt physically sick, knowing that he was presently witnessing thousands of men dying.

'How can you watch this,' Thomas asked the two men, 'and enjoy it like a day out in the country?'

'We came to watch our men destroying the Southern rednecks, my man,' the tall man said.

'It looks to me that they are losing,' Thomas replied, nodding his head towards the battlefield.

There was silence, and then another of the party joined them, 'Looks like our boys are in trouble, men. Maybe we should head home in case the Greycoats start heading north.'

The men muttered something under their breath and then drained their glasses. 'Probably right, Cyril. Wouldn't want to miss the train home.'

Thomas was in deep shock and couldn't believe that these respectable folks, their women in all their finery, had come all this way to watch a battle as entertainment!

They all packed away their picnic equipment and headed towards five carriages that were waiting for them.

'Where are you headed?' the short man asked Thomas.

Thomas could hardly speak. 'New York, sir.'

'Would you care for a lift, or are you going to walk there over the next month?' The tall man laughed.

Thomas nodded, as he knew this might be his only way of escape.

Chapter 13

Thomas stepped down off the train in New York station, but he couldn't even walk along the platform as it was packed with young soldiers waiting to board the train. He pushed his way towards the exit, but most of the men weren't interested in helping him as they were all in high spirits and wanting to get to the action. He finally made it to the back of the station, and was about to go through the huge front door when he heard someone calling him. He looked around but couldn't see anyone, so kept walking. A hand grabbed his shoulder. It was Colonel Arnold. 'Captain Sweeney, what are you doing here?' he barked.

Thomas turned and saw the wee man staring, puzzled, at him. 'Hello, Colonel, just got back from the South.'

'Yes I can see that, Captain, but why?' he asked crossly.

'I was captured by the Greycoats.' Thomas answered.

'Captured?' he shouted. 'How did you escape then, soldier?' the colonel asked with suspicion.

'I didn't. They let me go.'

'What?' shouted Colonel Arnold, 'No army lets a soldier go free during a war!'

'I spoke to them in Irish all the time and they thought I was crazy and, seeing as I had no weapon, they thought it would be easier just to let me go.'

'And what intelligence did you glean, Captain?' the colonel asked, getting more annoyed by the minute.

'Not much, Colonel, except that they are presently winning the first battle at Shenandoah Valley, and seem to be very well equipped.'

'See me in the morning, Captain,' Colonel Arnold shouted angrily, 'and give a full account of yourself,' He turned and stormed off.

Thomas turned and walked out of the station. All the military carriages and horses were in use, so he had to hire a private coach to take him home.

It was getting dark as he stepped off the coach at his front door. He was about to go into his house when he heard Mary shouting and running up their driveway, followed closely by Michael.

'Thomas,' she cried, as she fell into his arms. 'Oh my love I never thought I would see you again!'

'Steady now, girl. It's hard to kill a Donegal man.' Thomas picked her up and whirled her around a few times. Then he noticed Michael standing staring at him, so he went over to him to give him a big hug. 'Where have you two been, at this time of the evening?'

'I'll tell you later, Thomas,' replied Mary, making faces at him. 'Now it's time for a very big dinner.' They all went into the house, where Colleen ran to meet her da.

Mary was not long cooking a celebration dinner. They all joined hands and prayed before the meal and thanked God for Thomas's safe return.

They were nearly finished eating when Michael spoke up. 'Did you kill anyone, Da?'

Thomas was shocked, and stayed silent, looking at Michael for a few seconds before answering gently, 'No, Michael. I didn't kill anyone. I'm not a soldier and I didn't go off to fight.'

'Why not?' Michael asked, looking down at his plate.

'I was sent south to make maps, son. Maps that would help the soldiers find their way in unknown territory. That's all, Michael.'

Thomas was getting uncomfortable with his son's attitude, but realised that something had got to him.

'My friends went to fight for the freedom of America, Da.'

'Did they now, Michael? And what freedom would that be?' Thomas asked.

'Freedom for the black slaves Da, and so that our country may become one nation.'

'And where did you hear this, son?'

Michael went quiet, and then answered in a low voice,'A soldier came to speak at our school.'

Mary interrupted the conversation, as she was worried about Thomas finding out that Michael had tried to join the army. She would tell Thomas at a later time. 'Now who wants a big slice of my apple pie I made this morning?'

Joseph popped his head around the kitchen door just then, to make sure Colleen was all right and Mary thanked him for taking care of her.

Joseph was shocked and delighted to see Thomas, 'Oh master, it's so good to see you home. When I heard how bad things were for the soldiers, I thought you might have got caught up in it.'

'Thank you, Joseph. I'll tell you all before the week is out, and now I think we should all go to bed now that we're all full of apple pie. Would you like some, Joseph?'

'Thank you, master, but Colleen has been feeding me sweet things all evening, so yes, bed sounds good.'

'If you call me "master" one more time, Joseph, you won't have a bed to sleep in,' Thomas laughed, patting him on the back.

'Ok master, goodnight.'

The next morning was Saturday and Thomas was awake early. There was no sound from anyone else, so he slipped out to the back garden where he and Joseph had started making a large pond. It was more the size of a lake, Mary had said, and could hold a boat. Thomas was amazed that Joseph had finished it on his own, and it looked beautiful in the rising sun. Joseph had left a small island in the middle of it and Thomas could see about four ducks cleaning themselves at the water's edge. He took a deep breath and sat down on the seat that he had made before he left. 'God, that was a very strange outing,' he prayed as he soaked in the May sun. 'I am not sure what it was all about and what you want me to do with it, but I trust you to show me sometime, and thank you for bringing me home when so many young men will not get back to their homes.'

He felt Mary's hand on his arm and she sat down beside him.

'Was it bad, my love?' she asked quietly, staring out at the lake.

Thomas was slow to answer, 'No it wasn't, Mary. It was very strange. At times I was scared, then at times I sat back and watched God do strange things that I have no answer for.'

Mary snuggled up to him. 'You don't have to tell me, my love, unless you want to.'

Thomas began and told her the whole story of being captured and then let go because he helped the Confederates operate a new gun. He told her of watching thousands of soldiers killing one another, while a group of New York wealthy people had a picnic overlooking the battle, and how they brought him back to New York, which saved him walking one hundred miles.

Mary looked at him in disbelief and said with a worried voice, 'Does this mean the Confederates will win the war and we will have to flee.'

'I don't think so, as the Union still greatly outnumbers the Greycoats, but losing their first battle will make them take things more seriously.'

Mary was quiet for a while, then broke the news about Michael. Thomas was very quiet for a long time and Mary thought he was going to get very angry, but Thomas gave her a surprise reaction.

'I am very proud of him. That was a very courageous thing to do at fourteen, no matter what his motive. I must tell him how great he is.'

'But Thomas, if I had not gone straight to the barracks he would have gone on the train you just came off and we might never have seen him again.'

Thomas smiled at Mary, 'Now he wouldn't be the first person in our family to have the courage to go away now, would he?'

Mary looked at Thomas and took his face in her hands and kissed him hard on the lips.

'Why are you always right? It can be very annoying, but wonderful.'

'On Monday morning, I am going to the barracks to hand back my uniform.

'Oh Thomas, what an incredible man I married. I love you for ever,' she hugged him so tightly he groaned.

'I cant breathe girl. Are you trying to get rid of me that quick?' he laughed. He then took her hands and looked into her eyes. 'Maybe it's time we went back to Ireland.'

Mary's face lit up with a huge smile. She answered slowly, 'that would be my heart's desire, but we must ask God if that is what we should do.'

They walked hand in hand into the kitchen.

Chapter 14

They all went to church the next morning after a hearty breakfast, which Thomas cooked. The small white building was packed and the minister talked about the war and how God expected everyone to do their duty and join up to fight. Joseph and Charity came, and were taken aback by how friendly the people were to them. Thomas was not impressed as he could see people staring at him, and he knew they might be thinking that he was the only man of his age who wasn't away fighting.

As they were leaving. everyone shook hands with the minister. Thomas couldn't help himself. He could still see clearly the pictures of all the young men dying in the battle.'So Reverend,' he started politely, 'You are encouraging men to go and fight and die. What did Jesus say?'

The minister was shocked and went very quiet.

'The Bible I read says that Jesus said to love your enemies and do good to those who do you harm.'

'That's all very good, Mr Sweeney, but we must all defend our families,' replied the minister.

'That may be so, Reverend, if we are under attack, but our side are the attackers.'

Thomas didn't wait for a reply, as Mary pulled him down the steps.

'Thomas,' she scolded, 'There was no need to be unkind to the wee man. He doesn't know any better, and we are guests here.'

'Maybe, but there is no need for this war, and no need for Americans to kill each other.'

They climbed into their carriage and drove home in silence.

While Mary started cooking lunch, Thomas took Michael to the lake. 'I'm very proud of you, son,' he started. 'That was a very brave decision you made in attempting to sign up.'

Michael was very quiet and shocked, as he thought his father was going to tell him off.

'Why did you want to join the army, Michael?'

'A soldier from the Union army, came to our school and told us what the war was about and how we could make a difference, once we turned sixteen. He said the war was to set black slaves free in the South and to make America one country, where every man would be free and equal.'

Thomas sat looking out at the ducks on the pond, and pointed. 'Are those ducks free and equal, son? he asked, gently.

'What do you mean, Da?'

'Those ducks that are here every morning, son. They could easily fly over our fence and never come back.

Michael stared at them. 'So what you saying Da?'

'I'm saying, that things are not always what they seem. Those ducks chose to stay in our lake because we feed them and they feel secure here.

Michael said nothing for a while; then threw a pebble in the lake. 'This war is to set men free from slavery, Da.'

'It certainly is, Michael. No man should be a slave to another, and there are farms down south that make huge profits because they don't have to pay their workers.' Thomas paused, and then stood up beside Michael. 'Yet the workers don't run away, son, when they could, because many of them are well treated. They get housing and free food. The workers feel safer there than in a world such as we have here where, if you don't earn money, you don't eat.'

Michael looked at the ground.

'This war is not as clear as it seems, Michael. While it's good to free the black people from slavery, it's important to make sure that they will then will be well cared for and accepted into our community. To be honest, I can't see that happening here. President Lincoln also wants the country to be one, with a central government, which means a huge volume of wealth moving to those who may not even deserve it.'

'So why did you go to war, Da?' Michael replied sharply.

'I did not go to war, Son. I went to make maps.'

'Yes, but that was to help our soldiers fight against the enemy.'

'You are quite right, Son, and now I deeply regret it. I will be handing my uniform into the barracks tomorrow morning.'

Just then, Mary called them for lunch. 'I am still proud of your courage, Son, even though I think you made a bad decision.'

'I just wanted to be like you, Da,' Michael replied.

Thomas put his arm around him as they walked back to the house.

Monday morning was very warm in the May sunshine and, as Thomas was about to climb on his horse, Joseph passed by with a wheelbarrow full of soil.

'Joseph,' Thomas called, 'Hold your horses there.'

'Good morning, Master,' Joseph smiled.

'Where are you sleeping tonight?' Thomas asked, crossly.

'In my bed, I hope, Master,' Joseph replied, nervously.

'No, Joseph. You will have to find somewhere else to stay.'

Joseph looked shocked and dropped his eyes to the ground.

'I told you if you ever call me "Master" again, I would send you away,' Thomas scolded.

Joseph didn't know what to say, and muttered under his breath.

'What's my name, Joseph?' Thomas came up to him, and pulled his chin up.

'Thomas, Master,' Joseph muttered.

'Oh dear, Joseph, what am I going to do with you?' Thomas laughed, patting him on the back. 'You are free, Joseph and, while you work for me, you'll live as if you own this place. Now, what's my name?'

'Thomas,' Joseph said sheepishly.

'Well done, Joseph!' Thomas laughed heartily. With that, he climbed onto his horse.

'I'll be back shortly, Joseph, and then you and I have some planning to do.'

Thomas rode off down the driveway and Joseph continued with the wheelbarrow.

Thomas arrived at his barracks just as a large number of new young recruits were boarding wagons that would take them to the train station. He felt sad, thinking of how Michael could easily have been with them. He didn't wait to talk to anyone, but went directly around the back to the uniform store. It was empty with only one soldier behind the counter.

'You're too late, sir. All the uniforms are gone for today,' the soldier snapped.

'Well, you will be glad to see this one then,' Thomas said, as he dropped his kit onto the counter.

The soldier looked shocked and didn't know what to say.

'I won't need this any more,' Thomas said, as he walked out, 'It didn't fit me anyway.'

He was hoping he would make it back to his horse without meeting anyone, but just then Colonel Arnold came around the corner.

'Ah Captain, Sweeney,' he bellowed, 'Just the man I was looking for.'

'Thomas Sweeney, sir,' replied Thomas smiling, 'I'm no longer a captain as I have just resigned.'

'What?' shouted the colonel, 'Why did you do that?'

'Because I can, sir, and I just did. My enlistment was voluntary and casual, and I no longer want to be part of your unjust war.'

The colonel stopped and stared at him. 'I misjudged you, Sweeney. You are not the man I thought you were and, if you are serious, you will find life very difficult here when you walk out those gates.'

'I will not find life difficult, sir, as I am returning to Ireland. Life is much less complicated back home.'

The colonel turned and stormed off and Thomas walked to his horse and rode home.

Thomas was about to enter his driveway, when he noticed a big handmade sign posted on one of the gate pillars. "Blacks not wanted here. Go home!", the sign said. Thomas felt hot with rage. Tearing it down, he galloped to the front door. Mary was coming out with a neighbour who had come to visit her. 'Did you see this?' shouted Thomas, as he alighted from the horse.

He showed Mary the sign and she was shocked and upset as he was.

'Is Joseph alright?' Thomas asked, in a panic.

'Yes he is fine, Thomas. He's at the back feeding the ducks.'

Thomas went straight around to him at the back of the house.

'Joseph,' he called.

'Yes, Thomas,' answered Joseph, laughing.

'Good man, Joseph. You've got my name, at last. Listen, I wanted to ask you a very serious question and I hope you'll consider what I say very carefully.'

Joseph dropped the duck food and came over to him. Thomas asked him to sit beside him on the bench overlooking the lake.

'If you had the opportunity, Joseph, would you consider moving to another country, where race and colour do not matter?'

'Is there such a place sir?' replied Joseph, in a very sad voice.

'There is, Joseph. Back home, where we come from, people from other lands are rare, but they are well accepted. it's just that Mary and I are thinking of going home to Ireland and we would like you to come with us, as I mentioned to you before.'

Joseph looked alarmed. 'I could not imagine such a place, sir, and I couldn't leave Charity here in New York.'

'Joseph, do you think I would take you without your daughter?' Thomas scolded.

Joseph was very quiet, and was obviously thinking carefully about what to do.

'If you come to Ireland with us, Joseph, I will build you a small house beside mine and you can continue to work for me for as long as you wish. I will pay you well and you will be like one of the family. Michael and Colleen would be delighted to have you and Charity there, as well.'

'That is a very big decision, Thomas.' Joseph stared at the ground. 'It's very kind of you to ask me, and I'll talk to Charity tonight and think about it. I have never met a man so kind, sir, and America will be at a great loss without you.'

'I haven't told Mary yet, but I'll book our passage on the ship at the end of June, so you have a few weeks to make up your mind.' Thomas got up and patted him on the shoulder. 'You're a great man, Joseph.'

The next morning a policeman came to the door. Thomas opened it and invited him in.

'I believe you had a poster planted on your property, sir,' the policeman started. 'Do you still have it please?'

'I do officer,' Thomas replied, as he reached for it from the kitchen sideboard, 'It's an absolute disgrace.'

The policeman read it and rolled it up. 'Why do you think someone might have put this on your gate, sir?' the policeman asked.

'I don't know, officer, except that I employ a black gardener, who looks after my property.'

'There has been trouble down town, sir,' the policeman answered, as he moved to the kitchen door. 'The Irish in the city are protesting about Lincoln's intention to introduce conscription. It's not that they don't want to fight. It's because, at present, they can choose to fight for whoever offers them the best money. If conscription is brought in, then they have to fight for our Union army without pay, and they are mighty cross about it.'

'So why put this poster on our gate officer?' Thomas asked firmly.

'Some people see things very simply, sir, and blame the South for not co-operating with us, and they see black people as part of the problem. As I am sure you aware, that's not what it's all about, but that's what the newspapers print.'

'What do you suggest we do, officer?'

'You might be safer to get rid of your black worker, sir, so that your family is not made a target. There have already been a number of black people attacked within the city, and it won't be long before some innocent person is killed.'

'The black person you refer to, officer, is a friend of mine called

Joseph, and as long as we remain here, he will be welcome.' Thomas answered with anger.

The policeman touched his hat and turned to leave, 'It may be hard to protect your property, sir. We will do our best, but I would seriously reconsider your decision. Good day.'

Thomas watched him get into the police coach and drive away. He was so angry he didn't know what to do next. 'Mary,' he shouted, 'Where are you?'

Mary came around from the side of the house and could see that Thomas was more cross than she had seen him for a very long time.

'I'm going to town,' he shouted, 'Where's our carriage?'

Thomas went round to the right side of the house, where the stables were, and asked their driver to make the carriage ready. Mary was very worried, as she knew that he was capable of anything when his temper was roused about an injustice. She decided to go into the house and leave him for a while.

It was evening when Thomas returned from New York city, and Michael and Colleen were sitting with Mary drinking lemonade on the front veranda when the coach pulled up.

'Well how is my great family?' Thomas said with a big smile, as he approached them.

'Want some of Ma's lemonade, Da?' Colleen spoke first.

'Now how could I refuse the best lemonade in America,' as he hugged her, 'especially on this very important day?'

'What's so important today, Da?' Colleen laughed.

'Today I booked our tickets back to Ireland!' Thomas announced. 'We sail on the twenty first of June and will be back at home for the second week in July.'

'Why so soon?' Michael cut in. 'We are just getting used to our new life here.'

Thomas turned to Michael and sat beside him at the table. 'I know that, son, but life here could get very difficult for us, and we need to leave these folks here to fight their own war.'

Michael stood up and went into the house without saying anything.

'He'll come round, Thomas,' Mary said gently. 'He is trying to work everything out right now, and it's hard for a fourteen year old boy.'

Mary called them all for dinner, so they all went inside. Thomas knew that the next three weeks would be difficult.

Chapter 15

Two weeks later

The second week in June was very hot in New York that year. Michael and Colleen were enjoying playing by the lake, as Thomas was helping Mary pack their new things that they would take home to Ireland. Thomas came out the front door and was surprised to see a police coach coming up the driveway. 'Maybe they caught the person who put the poster on our gate,' Thomas thought, as he watched the policeman alight from the coach. He was surprised to see Lieutenant O'Hare step down behind the policeman.

'Hello, Lieutenant. Nice to see you,' Thomas said, walking towards them. 'I thought you had left the police to join the army.'

'I have, Thomas.' The Lieutenant dropped his eyes to the ground. 'It's just that the senior officer thought that I might be needed to bring you some sad news.'

Thomas stopped and looked very hard at the two of them. 'And what news might that be, sir?'

'This news concerns you gardener, I'm afraid'.

'Why? What happened?'

The two men could hardly speak, and shuffled nervously.

'I don't know how to tell this you, Thomas,' began the Lieutenant, 'I'm afraid he will not be going with you to Ireland. We found him dead this morning.'

Thomas couldn't speak and looked as if he were about to collapse, 'What do you mean?'

'He was found hanging from a street lamp, with two other black men.'

'What!' Thomas exclaimed getting very angry, 'How do you know it was Joseph?'

'He had documents on him with his address as this house, and when the sergeant saw the address, he knew that he was the man who worked for you.' Thomas went pale.

'I am so sorry, Thomas,' the Lieutenant added, 'This is an awful crime!.'

'Why did they pick on Joseph? He was the kindest soul anyone could meet.' Thomas waved his arms in exasperation. 'What is wrong with your country? How can I tell his daughter?' Thomas raged, as he walked towards the front door.

'Sir,' the policeman called, 'I'm afraid we will need you to come and identify the body, as there is no one else that we know of could do it.'

Thomas stopped and waved his arm. 'I will come later.' He slammed the door behind him.

Mary came from the kitchen and Thomas hugged her tightly, crying so hard he couldn't speak. Mary brought him into the kitchen and sat him down, while she made a cup of tea.

They sat for an hour holding hands and going over all the things they could have done to help Joseph and how they were going to tell the children. Joseph had told them that, after days of soul searching, he had decided that he would love them both to come to Ireland and start a new life as a truly free family. Thomas had planned with him what they would do to his new house in Donegal. They were going to extend the jetty at the bottom of the garden and make it into a small harbour that would take thirty foot fishing boats. They were also going to clear some of the trees at the back of the property and put in a large vegetable plot to grow cabbage and carrots.

Thomas was in a dream and just stared out the kitchen window. 'I have to go, and get this behind me,' he said sadly. 'I just do not know how I'll be able to do it. How are we going to tell Charity?'

'I don't know how, but I will try and tell her, with God's strength.'

'I would like to bury him in our garden. That's where he would be happiest.'

'Of course, my love. Go now and please do not say anything to annoy the police, as I am sure they are just as annoyed as you.'

Thomas didn't reply, but stood up and walked out towards the front door. He was about to call Joseph to ask him to get the driver to bring the coach, but stopped with a great sad sigh. He went around to the stables and asked the driver to saddle his horse.

When Thomas arrived at the local police station, he was surprised to see a number of soldiers standing about, and a few of them looked at him as he climbed up the wooden steps.

Lieutenant O'Hare was waiting for him, and gently escorted Thomas to a small room at the back of the station. 'I am so sorry, Thomas. I'm told that you treated this man very well and that he told so many of the local people what an unusually kind man you are.'

'Alfred, I am not unusual. I just believe that God made us all equal as far as race and colour go, and we all should be treated with respect.'

'We have found out it was gang of Irish people, who did this, Thomas, as they don't want President Lincoln to bring in conscription.'

'So why did they choose black people to hang?' Thomas replied, angrily.

'The war is about black people, so they chose targets that they knew would enrage the Union army.'

They came to the door and O'Hare opened it slowly and let Thomas go in first. The corpse was under a white sheet, and Thomas took a deep breath as O'Hare pulled it back to reveal Joseph's face. 'Its so unfair, Alfred. He was so looking forward to a new life with me in Ireland.'

Lieutenant O'Hare said nothing and Thomas put the sheet back. 'That is Joseph, my friend.'

They walked out of the station where Thomas mounted his horse.

'It's unlikely I will see you again, Thomas, as my unit ships out in the next few days,' O'Hare said, as he shook hands with Thomas. 'It has been an honour to meet you and your family,

Thomas and I hope that life back home will be the best you deserve.'

'Thank you, Lieutenant O'Hare. You have been a great help to us for a long time now, and I pray that you will survive the war and return safely to your family and friends.' With that, Thomas rode off.

Joseph's funeral was held in the small church, that the family had been attending. The minister was less than helpful, as there never had been a funeral for a black man in the church's history. Only about forty of the locals came, besides Thomas and the family. The minister didn't like the idea of Joseph being buried in his graveyard, so was quite relieved when he found out he was being buried in Thomas's garden. Michael and Colleen both cried for a long time, as they had become great friends with Joseph and Charity. Michael's attitude to the war changed completely when Thomas told him what had happened and what it was really all about.

Thomas noticed a black stranger at the graveside and, after Joseph was buried, he came over to him and Mary and shook their hands. 'You are fine people,' he started softly, 'Very fine. My friend, Joseph, never stopped talking about you. He was looking forward to his new life with you. it's a great tragedy that he never saw it, but then he never complained about anything in his life, and I'm sure he would be scolding in heaven if he knew we were blaming anyone for him being there early.'

Thomas stared at him with tearful eyes and took both his hands in his, 'Thank you, my friend.'

Michael and Colleen held hands with Charity. It seemed as if she would never be able to stop her tears from flowing. She was completely heartbroken.

Chapter 16

The next two weeks were very hard for the family. Thomas and Mary had to get the house ready to sell, when they were gone. The children were cruelly teased in school as the other children made remarks about their black slave being murdered. They were so upset that Mary kept them off for the last week before their departure. Colonel Arnold called at the house, to try and persuade Thomas to stay in the army. Thomas was polite but firm with him and told him he disagreed with his war. Someone had put another big painted sign on their gatepost saying, 'Cowards, run home.' It helped Thomas and Mary realise that going home was the best thing to do, and soon dispelled any regrets.

Thomas walked around the house to the back, to make sure everything was sorted for leaving. He found Charity sitting on the bench by herself, crying. Thomas sat down beside her and said nothing for a while, till she looked up at him.

'I don't know what to say, Charity.' Thomas started slowly. 'Your father was a remarkable man and did not deserve to die like this.'

'I can't live without my daddy. How will I ever cope in life without him?' Charity sobbed.

Thomas put his arm around her. 'We can never replace your mother and father, Charity, but Mary and I would like to adopt you and bring you with us to Ireland, as we had promised your father.'

'You are very kind, sir, and I love your family, but how can I live in a foreign land with no family of my own?' Charity took a handkerchief that Thomas handed to her and blew her nose.

'I can't promise it will be easy, but we have grown to love you in this short while, and we would love you to be part of our family in Ireland.'

Charity just stared at the ground for a long time. 'Then maybe I will come, sir.'

'On one condition, Charity,' Thomas smiled, standing up, 'You must never call me "sir" again.'

On the day of their departure, the driver arranged a coach and a wagon to take them all to the harbour. It was 7 AM when they left, as they were advised not to travel in the harbour area, from midday on as the protests started in the afternoons and went on till midnight.

Thomas and Mary didn't even look back as their carriage went down their drive for the last time.

'I made a mistake in bringing us here, Mary. I never asked God for His direction, and I'm sorry,' Thomas took Mary's hand and stroked it gently.

'Never say that, Thomas. We have learned a lot in our short time here, and someday good will come of it.'

Michael and Colleen sat on the opposite side of the coach and they watched their parents very carefully. 'We have grown up, Da,' Michael said, smiling at his father. 'We will never see things in the same way. it's good we came.'

Colleen just nodded and Thomas felt very proud of them.

As their coach came near to the harbour they could see some of the side streets where shops had been burned and carriages overturned.

'The rioting seems to have been very bad. They have wrecked some of the streets.'

'It's embarrassing to think it's Irish people who have done this, Thomas, just because they want to be paid to fight.'

'Our people came over here to find a better life, but end up destroying what is already here.' Thomas sighed. He decided to change the subject.

'We're going on a brand new ship, folks.'

'What does that mean?' asked Michael.

'It's an iron steam ship, and will cut the crossing time to under two weeks. It's bound for Glasgow, in Scotland, but will stop at Moville.'

'Will we have a cabin, Da?' asked Colleen excitedly.

'You will have your own cabin, and it even has a dining room where you can have scrumptious meals on the way over,' Thomas replied.

Just then the coach arrived at the harbour and, just as Thomas had said, there was a huge black ship, with people already boarding. As they got out of the coach, they were surrounded with men in uniform, lifting cases and checking tickets. There was a strong smell of the sea, and smoke coming from the ship's funnels. Charity had never seen anything like the ship in her life and was both amazed and scared. Michael and Colleen took it in turns to hold her hand.

Thomas showed his tickets to one man and asked why was the ship not so busy, upon which he was told that the ship was on its return journey and had very few passengers but instead. carried a lot of cargo. They said goodbye to the drivers as all their luggage seemed to disappear further down the quay to where a crane was lifting boxes on board. Thomas and Mary made their way to the cabin deck and made sure all their tiny cabins were together.

'When the ship's horn blows, who would like to say goodbye to America?' Thomas asked.

Michael and Colleen replied that they wanted to explore the ship with Charity, and Mary decided to stay in the cabin and sort through all the clothes that they had brought with them. Thomas left them and made his way to the deck overlooking the harbour. He stood in silence, watching all the busy men loading the ship and was unaware of the captain coming up behind him.

'It's quite a scene,' the captain said, in a friendly tone. Thomas looked round in surprise.

'I'm sorry, sir. I didn't see you there. I was in a daydream, 'Thomas responded, looking nervously at the captain.

'Not a lot of people making your journey,' the captain continued.

'No, I guess not, sir. With that uniform, may I presume that you are the captain?'

'Something like that. And you? Are you a professional man?'

'I don't know what I am, Captain. I came here six months ago to start a new life, but it seems to have gone in the wrong direction.'

'I see many people on my ship who make the same journey, thinking America is the answer to all their troubles and the fulfilment of their dreams, but from what I see, it's not everyone who finds life that way.'

'That's very sad, Captain.' Thomas sighed.

'it's, but still they come, and I hear recently that we have carried over a million passengers over the last ten years, and many of ones that went in the early years didn't even survive the journeys They died of sickness and disease.'

'The famine destroyed Ireland, Captain. I wonder if it will ever recover,' Thomas remarked sadly.

'What sends you back, sir?' the captain asked quietly, as he filled his pipe and lit it.

'I am a wealthy man, Captain, and I had no need to leave my country. I came to fulfil a selfish dream of becoming a famous inventor,' Thomas said, with a sigh.

'Well then, may I say that Ireland needs you more than America and, when you go home, by fulfilling your dream there you might improve the life of your people at home.' The captain turned to walk away.

'Thank you, Captain, I will listen to that advice. God bless your new ship.'

He walked further down the deck and as he heard the ship's horn blow. Within a few minutes, the ropes were loosened and she slowly slipped out of New York harbour.

Thomas went looking for the children.

The first two days of the crossing the sea were calm but, by the third day, an unusual summer storm blew up and the ship rolled badly, making them all sea-sick. It only lasted for two days and the rest of the journey was reasonable. Thomas and Mary talked a lot about their adventure, for the first few days, till they both said, 'What will we do now?' This was the first time in Thomas's life that he had no direction and no purpose, other than to raise his family, and it bothered him. He lay awake at night staring at the cabin ceiling wondering what being at home would be like, especially when neighbours found out that he had failed in America.

The day before the ship came to the Donegal coastline the captain knocked on Thomas's cabin door.

'Hello, Captain,' Thomas said with curiosity.

'Captain Thomas Sweeney?' the captain enquired, knowingly.

Thomas went white. 'It would appear that you have annoyed a lot of important people back in America. He paused and showed Thomas a piece of paper. 'I received this urgent telegram, asking me if were you on board my ship and, if so, I was to return to New York and hand you over to the police. The message explains that during the battle at Shenandoah Valley, which the Union army lost, by the way, they captured an Irish Confederate soldier who, in return for not being shot or imprisoned, informed them that one of their own men had shown the confederate army how to use a new automatic gun which killed thousands of their men. The soldier named the person as you.'

Thomas read down the sheet and confirmed everything the captain had just said. There was silence between them, and then the captain started to laugh.'I have no intention of turning my ship back to New York, as I have no "Thomas Sweeney" on my ship.'

Thomas was speechless for a few seconds. 'Did they give the name of the Confederate soldier whom they captured.'

'No I think not, but now I can see now why you are returning to Ireland.'

'It's not what it seems, Captain,' Thomas started to explain, but the captain stopped him.'

'Listen, Mr Sweeney, it's none of my business what you did, or to whom you did it. If you helped develop a weapon that shortens a war, then you did well.'

'I didn't support any side, Captain. I hate war, but it was a deal I agreed to just to get released so I could see my family again. I'm sure they would have worked out how to use the weapons themselves. It just might have taken a bit longer.'

'Good man, Mr Sweeney. From what I hear the war which they have started might be the downfall of the entire country. It means, though, that you can never return, or they will string you up as a traitor.'

'Get some sleep, sir. We'll be approaching Ireland in the morning and no one will ever know about this note. I will probably have to skip a voyage or two next month, but sure, I'm due a holiday anyway.'

Thomas closed the door, as Mary woke up and wanted to know

what the captain wanted.

'Just a friendly chat, Mary, and to let us know we'll be in Donegal at noon tomorrow.'

The family had just finished a late breakfast when, out of the window, they could see Ireland in the distance. Thomas took a deep breath and announced 'Thank God! We're home again!'

Mary suggested that they all go out on deck for the last hour of the journey. It wasn't as warm in Ireland, and the sky was grey, but Thomas was pleased to hear the sound of the seagulls.

Mary put her arm through Thomas's and hugged him tightly. 'I am so glad to be home, Thomas. I never want to leave Ireland again.'

'We never shall, Mary. We never shall!' he said, stroking her hair. 'I hope John got my message to meet us at the boat.'

Mary laughed, 'I wouldn't care if I had to walk all the way home.'

'Yes, but I would,' Michael chipped in.

John was waiting for them, as they climbed out of the small tender at Moville harbour.

'Hello, my family. How great to see you,' he shouted over the small group of men waiting to unload cargo.

'How great to see you too, John.' Thomas hugged him.

'Look at the size of this young man and woman,' John said, turning to Michael and Colleen, 'And my favourite Donegal girl,' as he picked up Mary and gave her a twirl.' And who might this beautiful young woman be?'

'This is Charity, John. She's my new daughter and is coming to live with us.' Mary said smiling.

'You're most welcome to Ireland, Miss Charity. We need a new person to cheer us up around here.' John laughed.

They never stopped talking all the way back to Greencastle, as Thomas related some of his story to John, without telling him about his capture by the Confederates. The afternoon sun came out as they approached the gates of the house and Thomas felt like running up the driveway. He was so pleased to be home.

'I didn't get much done in six months, but I built you a new gate at the front of the house,' John said proudly.

'I see it, John. It looks a bit posh.' Thomas replied as their coach arrived at their front door.

Chapter 17

It took Thomas and Mary a few days to adjust to being back home. The weather in July improved and it was warm enough for them all to enjoy being by the sea again. The fourth day home, they all went and visited Thomas and Mary's mothers, and had a tearful reunion. Rose and Bridget were astonished to meet Charity. They never once made a comment on her colour but went out of their way to make her feel at home. Thomas was surprised that the dirt tracks were being replaced by properly made roads, which were levelled and then rolled to make them safer and more comfortable. They decided that after the trauma of the visit to America, they would spend the summer relaxing, before planning the next adventure.

When they got back to their house in Greencastle, John was waiting for them.

'I found this letter for you, Thomas, but it was sent to my address. It looks somewhat fancy, so I didn't dare open it.' John handed it to Thomas as the rest of the family went into the house. 'It came a few weeks ago and when you told me you were coming home, I thought I would keep it.'

'Thanks, John,' said Thomas, opening the envelope carefully. 'Mmm, it's from my estate in England, and signed by Richard.' Thomas read the letter quietly. Then turned to John. 'Well, goodness me, that's some sad news! Richard's wife, Ann, has left him.'

'Oh dear, poor Richard,' exclaimed John 'When did this happen?'

'Looking at the date on this letter it must have been a few months ago. This is shocking! The poor man must be distraught.'

'She seemed a very nice girl. I thought they were very happy.' John walked up and down.

Thomas looked sad and stared out at the sea. 'I must go to him. He's my best friend and was very kind to me when I lost Christina. This is not good.'

'New railways have been built all over the country since you left, and there's a new ship crossing from here to England, so it will be a lot easier now to get to him.' John said.

'Good. Could I ask you, please, to book my journey for me while I go and tell Mary. I'm a little unsettled right now, and the idea of going away again doesn't hold well with me.'

'Leave it all to me, Thomas. I would say at this stage it will be next week before you get a ticket, as it only sails three days a week..'

Thomas smiled gratefully and turned and walked into his house, calling Mary. She was coming down the stairs when he found her. 'Ann has left Richard,' he told her. 'The poor man is distraught.'

'Oh no!' exclaimed Mary, 'They seemed so happy together. What happened?'

'His letter just said that he found her gone one day and a note stating she could no longer live with him,' Thomas said sadly.

Mary was quiet for a while, and then turned to Thomas, 'You need to go to him, Thomas.'

'I will. I was just going to ask you if I could do that very thing,' Thomas replied.

'I will go into Moville and send a telegram to tell him I will be with him shortly.'

Mary tried to make the next few days as normal as possible, as she knew this would be a hard trip for Thomas. Not only would he be with his best friend, who was so distressed, but he would also be back in his former house, where Christina died. John booked the tickets for Thomas for the following Tuesday, reassuring Thomas that the new rail network meant that, for most of his journey, he would have the comfort of a train instead of a horse-drawn carriage.

'What will I say to him?' wondered Thomas, as he paced up and down the living room.

'Maybe you could find Ann and see if you could talk sense into her. There must be some secret reason that she would leave such a happy life,' Mary said, as she helped Colleen fit on a new dress.

What do you think, Da?' Colleen said, as she spun around in the dress Mary had bought for her in New York. 'There won't be any clothes like this here.'

Thomas smiled 'You look amazing, Colleen, and growing into a beautiful young woman far too quickly.'

'Maybe you'll bump into Queen Victoria on your travels. I hear she's coming to Ireland next week.' Mary said, laughing.

Thomas looked at Mary with a puzzled look. 'She will be going to Dublin and not near where I will be.

'We need to find out what has been happening to our country while we have been away.' Mary said, as she walked out of the room.

'It's more important, my love, that we try and persuade both our mothers to let me build them a house next door so we can look after them, now that they are getting older.'

'I will try again while you are gone, but I don't hold out much hope.'

Michael came in the front door with his boots on and a fishing rod in his hand, 'You coming, Da, or am I away again on my own?'

'Give me a few minutes, Michael, and I will be with you. Sure it's a nice day. Why don't we take the boat out for a short run? We can maybe catch some mackerel further out,' Thomas said as he went to change.

The sea was very calm and the sun was hot, as they pushed the boat out from the shore.

'Joseph and I had plans to build a new harbour here, son, it's so sad that he never saw any of his new life.'

'It's very sad, that he has gone, Da, but I'm still here and I could help you build the new pier.'

'Would you?' asked Thomas, with surprise.

'Of course I would. We could start now and finish it by next spring,' Michael replied, as he fixed some bait to his fishing line.

'We could that,' Thomas laughed, 'but right now we need to catch a few fish for dinner.'

They had been fishing for about an hour, when Michael suddenly turned to his Da and said, 'Tell me about my grandfather, whom I never knew, Da, and how he drowned.'

Thomas was shocked and totally unprepared for his son ever asking that question. He sat staring at the water for a long time.

'Your grandfather was a very kind, hard-working man, son,' Thomas started slowly. 'He was a great inventor, but never had the money to put his ideas into practice. He invented a new part for our plough which made it slice through the ground more easily and which meant we could do far more ploughing in a day. His real love was fishing, though, and that's why he became good friends with Mary's father, Fergal, who owned a curragh boat. They would spend days at sea, and caught loads of fish. Then came a bad winter, and they couldn't get out in the flimsy boat, and so had no fish to sell in the market. With no sales, it meant he had no income and my da soon went behind on his rent. The day of the accident was the start of the new fishing season and they took me with them as a birthday present. It was a day like today, but a storm came in from the west suddenly and, despite our two das rowing hard, they could not make it back to shore before a huge wave overturned the boat. I was the only survivor. Within a month the bailiff came and put us out of our house because Ma couldn't pay the rent, and that's why your two grandmothers now live together.'

Michael was very silent and sat chewing dulse. 'I would love to have known them. Life seems too unfair.'

'They were great men, but right now they would be very annoyed if they thought that we were looking back, when we have so much life in front of us.'

'I know, Da,' said Michael sadly. 'The problem is, I'm like you, and I want to do more with my life than grow potatoes.'

Thomas laughed, taking the oars and turning the boat for home. 'And so you shall, young man, for I haven't even started yet, at thirty seven, and I'm going to need a strong son to work with me.'

As the boat crunched onto the stony shore, Thomas said, 'Michael, I have to go and visit Richard next week as he is in trouble. I will only be gone a couple of weeks, so I need you to look after your ma and sister.'

'The last time you left us, Da, you were on a secret mission to help the American army. I hope you aren't going to do anything stupid this time.'

'Listen to the pup calling me stupid,' Thomas laughed 'and who was going off to fight at the age of fourteen?'

Mary and the children came to the gate to see Thomas onto the coach to Derry. John was there also, with all the tickets.

'That's the lot Thomas. I even booked you first class on the ship and train, but I would doubt that will make much of a difference,' he laughed, giving Thomas a large envelope. 'Queen Victoria is coming to Ireland while you are away, so maybe you'll bump into her on your travels.'

'I hope not, John, as I am not well pleased with our government right now. I'm starting to think like some of our neighbours that it's time we governed our own country.'

'I thought you were a great supporter of the English. What has brought about your change of mind?' John asked, concerned.

'The way London responded to the famine was shocking, and I've heard that they could easily have saved millions of lives if they had reacted sooner and with more compassion.'

Thomas picked up Colleen and gave her a big hug. 'This is not the time for politics. Some day it will all work out, won't it, my love?'

The coach arrived and Thomas climbed in with Mary and Michael amid a chorus of "Good luck" and "God bless you". They stood and watched the coach disappear towards Moville.

Chapter 18

The journey took nearly three days, and when Thomas's train pulled in at the station near his estate, he was filled with memories and emotions. He remembered that this was the station that he and Richard had pulled into sixteen long years ago and were met by the pompous chauffeur who worked for Lord Shrewsbury. The two of them were like little boys at the time and were totally gobsmacked at the size and elegance of the house. Thomas would never have believed that, due to tragic circumstances, one day he would inherit the estate after having married the lord's daughter, Christina, only to lose her so soon in childbirth.

As the train came to a stop, Thomas continued sitting. He wasn't looking forward to having all these memories come back to him. He jumped out of his seat when he heard the guard blow his whistle for the train to leave again. The train was actually moving when he jumped with his bag onto the platform, almost knocking Richard to the ground.

'There you are, my Irish friend,' Richard laughed, 'I thought you had missed your train, or gone on to Scotland.'

Thomas gave Richard a big hug, 'How are you, my friend?'

Richard cleared his throat, 'Well, I could be better, Thomas, but I'll tell you all when we get home.'

The carriage brought them up the long drive to the estate house, where the lights were all on, and a butler was waiting for them at the front door, 'I see you're still living in style,' Thomas smiled.

'Keeping up your standard,' replied Richard, as they walked in the front door.

Thomas's heart was pounding as he expected to see Christina come running downstairs to meet him, and he stopped to take a deep breath.

'I know this will be exceptionally hard for you, and I deeply appreciate you coming to see me, but let's try and remember the fun we had here and not just the sad times.'

The butler came and took their coats and told them that dinner was served in the dining room. Every room had a memory of Christina in it, and Thomas felt like going straight home, but he knew that his friend needed him.

'This is the room where we first met Lord Shrewsbury. He came bounding in that door full of life and fun to meet with two young opportunists.'

'We were professional surveyors, and you must not forget that it was we who changed this estate from a sinking ship into a very prosperous place where many people would dream of living.'

'But not Ann,' Thomas said gently, as they took their seats. 'Have you heard from her?'

Richard looked very troubled as he tucked his napkin onto his lap.

'No not a word. I came down for breakfast one morning and this note was on the mantelpiece.'

Thomas read the short not that simply said 'Goodbye, Richard, my love. I cannot live with the pretence any more. Ann.' 'This is very strange, Richard, I thought she was very happy here with you.

'One of my friends in our local pub told me that Ann had confided in her that she could never tell me the reason for her leaving,' Richard said, pacing up and down.

'There is a mystery here, Richard, that needs unfolding,' Thomas said, thoughtfully.

'I just don't understand,' continued Richard, 'We met in a pub about ten miles from here and, within an hour of chatting, we both knew we had met someone special. I arranged to meet down by a river one afternoon and it was there I asked her to marry me. She had no idea who I was or where I lived, so she seemed unimpressed when I eventually told her that I lived in the Shrewsbury estate.'

'Strange indeed, my friend. 'I think there is more to this than meets the eye.'

He could see that Richard was at the point of crying, so he lightened the conversation till they finished their dinner.

Richard showed Thomas to one of the guest rooms after they had chatted for hours, but they had to pass the room where Thomas and Christina had slept, and where she had died. Thomas opened the door and stared in.

'Come on, friend,' Richard pulled him away from the door. 'That room will never be used again, and there's no point in giving yourself more pain.'

Although he was tired, Thomas could hardly sleep, knowing that down the corridor was the room where he and Christina had made love as husband and wife for a year, and where she took her last breath. He deeply loved his wife Mary but still could not forget Christina.

The next morning, Thomas and Richard met in the same dining room for breakfast and Thomas announced he had a plan. 'I don't believe that Ann left because of her life here, and I intend to get her back for you.'

Richard looked shocked, as he ate his eggs, and said nothing.

'Where's the pub that you met Ann in? I must go there today.'

'What on earth for?' asked Richard.

'I have a plan,' Thomas replied, 'Now when we are finished you must take me on a walk around the house.'

Richard took Thomas out the back door first to show him the new stables and the fine array of horses. 'I see you've knocked the old stables down,' Thomas said, pointing at the big shining new row of stables.

'Yes, they were in a bad state,' Richard answered nervously.

'That was where Christina and I first kissed.' Thomas said, looking at Richard.

'That is why I knocked it down,' laughed Richard, 'One less memory of Christina to get you down.'

'I'm not down, but when you loved someone as much as I loved her I will never forget, and Mary will never replace her.' Thomas walked on.

'You know then how I feel now without my Ann,' Richard said, sadly.

'Yes I do, my friend, only Ann isn't dead, and I will get her back for you.' Thomas smiled.

'How?'

'I told you I have a plan, and it starts tonight,' Thomas smiled. Richard shrugged his shoulders and walked off.

They walked around the back gardens, which were full of fruit trees and vegetable plots, before coming around to the front of the house where the fountains were splashing in the summer sun.

Thomas stared at the fountains, remembering that it was Christina who designed them, and that this was where he proposed to her.

Richard stood beside him and stayed silent, knowing just how hard this must be for him. They both stood for a good twenty minutes before Thomas spoke first. 'I need a pint of your English ale. I've seen enough of sadness for one day.'

They walked up to the picnic area at the side of the house and asked the butler to bring them a drink.

It was late afternoon when Thomas's coach stopped outside the pub. It seemed very quiet.

Thomas went up to the bar where one older man was cleaning glasses. 'Good day, sir,' Thomas started, 'I was looking for a friend of a friend and was wondering if you could help me find her.'

The man just looked at Thomas with suspicion and then said slowly, 'Maybe, depends.' He kept cleaning the glasses.

'My good friend met a young lady here, over a year ago, and was wondering if she still frequents your establishment.'

'We get lots of young ladies in here, sir. What's the attraction with this one?' he asked curiously.

'They were very close for a while and then she seemed to disappear, and he's worried about her.' Thomas continued.

'If your friend is that worried about her why did he not come here himself?' the barman asked, in a dismissive tone.

'He is, in fact, looking in a large number of places for her, and so I am helping him.' Thomas turned to look around the pub. 'The lady's name is Ann Parker.'

The barman looked at him for a long time before he said with disdain, 'I don't let that type in here, any more. You need to go down the street and take the first alley to the right. You will find a very run down hotel – but it's not a hotel, if you know what I mean. It's where she hangs out along with a few other girls.'

Thomas was shocked, and didn't need any further explanation. He thanked the barman and walked back out onto the street. This is not good, he said to himself, as he took a breath of the summer air. How will I explain this to Richard? He decided that he would go and check out the hotel. The alleyway was filthy, and a drunk man was lying asleep against one of the doors. A large dog appeared, growling and chasing a very thin cat that disappeared into a disused barn. Thomas knocked on the door. There was no answer for about five minutes and he was about to turn and walk away when an older woman opened the door.

'Sorry to bother you, ma'am. I am looking for a girl called Ann Parker. Just wondering if she might be in.'

'Wait there till I see if she has a client.' The woman slammed the door shut again.

Thomas had no idea how he was going to cope with this if she actually agreed to see him. The woman opened the door again and said. 'She is upstairs in room three. Show us your money first.'

Thomas was about to say he didn't require her services, but then decided to pull out a pile of money from his pocket, and the woman showed him the stairs.

Thomas climbed the stairs and walked along a very dreary long corridor till he came to room three. He knocked the door and went in. Ann was sitting on a bed in her underclothes and was counting money. Startled, she looked up at Thomas. She leapt off the bed and pulled a blanket around her. 'What are you doing here?' she yelled.

'It's ok, Ann. I'm not here for your services,' Thomas said quietly.

'How did you find me? Does Richard know I am here?' She was almost crying.

'The pub landlord told me you might be here and, no, Richard does not know.'

Ann sat down on the bed again, with tears in her eyes. 'How is he, sir? I can't remember your name, even though I stayed in your house a year ago,' she sobbed.

'My name is Thomas. Richard could be better, Ann, as he's beside himself with worry about you.' Thomas answered quietly.

Ann started crying. 'I didn't want to leave him. I loved him very much, and still love him, but I was afraid that he would find out some day what trade I was in before I met him and that he would be disgusted and throw me out publicly.'

'Well, Ann,' Thomas started in a comforting voice. 'You do not know my best friend very well yet, for he would have nothing but compassion and kindness for you, as I do.'

'He thought so highly of me, after meeting me in the pub, and everything went very quickly. He had me moved to the house and bought me new clothes, and never once asked me what I was doing on my own in the pub.' Ann was now crying into her hands. 'I can never go back to him now because I'd have to tell him the truth.'

Thomas knelt on one knee and took her head in his hands and gently wiped her tears away with his handkerchief. 'My wife was in the same business in New York. She was kidnapped and forced into it. When I found out, I had to come to terms with it. That life was not what she wanted, as I believe this is not what you want either.'

Ann shook her head, 'I hate it and I would rather kill myself, than keep living this life.'

'Well today it ends,' Thomas said, standing up. 'God has sent me to rescue you and bring you back to Richard.'

'I can't, sir, as much as I want to be free. I could never look at my husband again,' she said sadly, 'And your God would not want me either.'

Thomas gently made her stand up. 'Get dressed. Let me talk to

Richard. I know he will be so pleased to see you and will understand your situation.'

Ann stood in front of a mirror, still crying, and was trying to decide what to do. 'Wait for me downstairs while I get dressed,' she sobbed.' You will have to pay my madam as you are leaving or she will cause a big row. I will tell her I am going to the pub for a break and hopefully she'll believe me.'

'Will you come back with me then?' Thomas asked her, gently.'

She paused for a few seconds, looking at the floor. 'Yes,' She whispered, 'But we need to be quick.'

Thomas paid his money to the woman and walked out the door. He waited at the top of the alley, not sure that Ann would come, but was pleased when she ran towards him. 'We need to go quickly as she often checks on us going to the pub,' Ann said in a panic. They walked quickly back to the carriage which was outside the pub, and raced off as soon as she got in.

It was getting dark by the time the carriage pulled up at the front of the estate door, and Thomas told Ann to wait in the carriage. He handed his coat to the butler and asked where Richard was. 'He is in the drawing room, sir,' The butler replied. 'He has been sitting staring at the fire all evening.' Thomas walked in quietly and stood behind him. 'A penny for your thoughts, my old friend.'

Richard jumped. 'I didn't hear you come in, Thomas. I was thinking'

Thomas picked up a glass of whiskey. 'How many of these have you had while I was away looking for your wife?'

'Quite a few, as I knew you would never find her,' Richard replied, sadly. Thomas knelt down beside Richard and smiled. 'She's in the carriage.'

Richard jumped out of the chair, 'What! You found her? Where?'

'Yes. She's found', Thomas replied, happily. 'I'll tell you shortly'.

Richard ran towards the door, but Thomas grabbed him by the arm. 'No, Richard. She only agreed to come back if I tell you her story, as she won't do it herself.'

Thomas asked the butler to bring Ann into the other living room and give her some food, while he took nearly half an hour talking to Richard.

By the end of their conversation, Richard was in tears. Thomas went to speak with Ann.

'Richard is heartbroken for you, Ann, as I knew he would be, and says he loves you even more,'

Thomas said, holding Ann's two hands in his. 'You will have to learn to let the past go, and know that you have an incredible future here in this beautiful home. You are married to one of kindest men in England, who loves you beyond words, and he's waiting for you now. I'll say goodnight now and let you talk on your own.'

Ann got up and hugged Thomas, kissing him on the cheek. 'I know now why Richard always spoke so highly of you. I will always be so grateful to you.'

Thomas went to bed and Ann went in to talk with Richard.

Chapter 19

Breakfast was late the next morning, and no one was in a hurry to get up. Thomas was the first to appear in the breakfast room, and the sun was already pouring in the tall windows.

'Good morning, sir,' the butler said, as Thomas picked up a newspaper. 'Will you want a full breakfast today?'

'Yes please, and you can bring in the other two as well. If it gets cold, it will serve them right for sleeping in on such a beautiful day.' Thomas sat at the head of the table.

'Very good, sir. I'll bring a pot of tea straight away,' the butler said, as he was about to leave the room.

'Just a minute', Thomas called after him, 'When did you last have a day off?'

The butler seemed a bit awkward and muttered, 'Don't rightly know, sir.'

'I'll be mentioning to Richard to let the staff off today so they can enjoy the sunshine.

The butler looked alarmed, but pleased, nevertheless.

The butler left and Thomas opened the newspaper to see the headlines stating that Queen Victoria was in Ireland. 'Come to see what a mess her government had made of the famine crisis,' thought Thomas. 'I wonder will she be told the truth.'

Just then Richard and Ann strolled in, arm in arm. 'Well look at the love birds,' Thomas laughed. 'I ordered your breakfast.'

Richard and Ann sat down at the table and were unusually quiet. Thomas kept reading the paper, before he announced, 'I want to go to the dam today and I think you two should come with me.'

Richard looked at him and turned to Ann, 'I think we owe him that.'

'You owe me nothing, except I have just suggested you give all your staff the day off today.'

'What? Why, Thomas? We need them.' Richard was alarmed.

'No we don't, Richard, and your butler couldn't remember the last time he had a day off. Do we really need butlers, for that matter? It's about time we started doing things for ourselves.'

Richard was quiet, but Ann was laughing to herself as she buttered her toast.

'I would like to take a trip to Bristol after we go the dam, and I thought we could stay in a hotel tonight and take a leisurely journey home tomorrow.' Thomas smiled as he folded up the paper.

Richard looked at him as if he had lost his mind, but said nothing.

They arrived at the dam at midday, and the reservoir looked splendid in the summer sunshine. Thomas was so pleased to see that his dream was working well and that nature had turned it into a place where many visitors came to spend a day out with peace and quiet. Thomas left Richard and Ann by the coach as he went to the water's edge to stare across the valley. He remembered standing here with Lord Shrewsbury as they discussed Thomas's seemingly insane plan to flood the valley. He was shocked when the lord agreed with his idea and gave him permission to make it work. Tears came to his eyes again, as he was very fond of his late father-in-law who gave a lot of his life to trusting Thomas. Giving Thomas his daughter, Christina, was the greatest gift in the world, and Thomas was still heartbroken that the lord never got to see how happy their marriage was when he died in the coach crash. He looked down the road, remembering that day when this scene was one of the last sights the lord saw before he died.

'Many memories,' Richard said, as he came up beside him.

'We have had a great life, but it's sad to think that it has been at the expense of two amazing people,' Thomas said sadly.

'That's so true, but neither of them would have liked to have seen us today standing here being sad,' Richard replied, picking up a small stone and throwing it into the lake.

'Lets go to Bristol, then,' Thomas said, patting Richard so hard on the back that he nearly fell into the lake.

The two of them climbed the grass bank back up to the coach where Ann was enjoying sitting in the sun. The coach set off for the long journey to Bristol.

Two days later

It was mid afternoon when they arrived back at the house, and they were all full of chatter about what an amazing city Bristol was. They had enjoyed going to the spa and visiting the new Bristol suspension bridge, which was nearly completed. The city was full of life, with many pubs and eating houses, all full of wealthy people from London. As the coach stopped at the front door, the butler appeared. 'A telegram came for you yesterday, sir, but as I didn't know where you were, I was unable to forward it to you.'

'Thank you, Arthur,' replied Richard, opening and quickly reading it.

'Oh goodness,' Richard shouted, 'It's from Lord Shrewsbury's brother, Sir Henry. It says he is arriving for a visit tomorrow – no wait – this arrived yesterday. That means he's arriving today! Oh dear, we must run to get ready.'

'Don't panic, Richard,' Thomas laughed 'The house is fine and he's probably in the area and wants to see how you are getting on.'

The three of them walked into the house and Richard starting barking orders to all the staff. They were shocked when, just then, a very expensive coach pulled up at the front door.

'Oh no,' shouted Richard. 'He's here!'

'Leave this to me,' laughed Thomas. 'Go and get changed while I entertain him.'

Thomas went out to the coach where Sir Henry was stepping out of the coach, with great difficulty. 'Great to see you, Henry.'

'Oh goodness me! Is that really you, Thomas? I thought you were living in Ireland now.'

'I am indeed, sir, but I came over to check that Richard was keeping the place up to your standard,' he said, shaking hands with Henry.

'No problem there, Thomas,' smiled Henry. 'He has done a sterling job of making the estate one of the few that are paying its way in England. He's a great young fellow.'

Sir Henry took Thomas's arm and hobbled into the house. Thomas was shocked at how frail he had become. It was only sixteen years since they last met, and Thomas had calculated that Henry would only be about seventy five.

'Please come in and sit down, sir, while I order tea,' Thomas said, making signs to the butler.

'Richard will be with us in a few minutes.'

'Thank you,' Henry said, as he sat on one of the soft seats. 'I always get sad coming here, son, when I think of my late brother leaving this place so early in life, and then his daughter never getting to enjoy it either. Life can be so unfair, can't it?'

'Indeed it can, sir. Even though I'm remarried, I still find it impossible to forget Christina and the short, wonderful time we had together.'

'She used to write to me, son.' He paused, looking at the floor. 'I never told you this, as it was a secret between us. When her father died, she went through that terrible time of depression. She came to me and asked if I would be a father to her. She wanted to know if she could write to me but that I was not to reply in case you opened one of the letters. She also asked me not to tell you as she didn't want to worry you.'

Thomas was very silent for a while and then asked, sadly. 'And what did my wife write to you about, uncle?'

'Most of the letters were about you. She kept telling me that she had found the only real gentleman in England and that she was bursting with happiness.'

Thomas shook his head and took out a handkerchief. He could hardly contain his tears.

You made her life perfect, son, and I don't know why life took it away from her so soon. It seems so cruel.'

Thomas was now crying openly. He stood up and walked to the window, staring at the fountain that Christina had designed. 'It would appear, uncle, that God must have needed her more than me. as I am sure she is even happier now,' Thomas choked.

'Maybe, but I just wished my brother could have seen how happy you made her.'

Richard came in to the room and went over and shook Henry's hand. When he saw them both so upset he went and sat down quietly.

The butler arrived with tea, which lightened the atmosphere, and small chat ensued between them. When tea was finished, Henry coughed hard. Thomas jumped to see if he was alright.

'I came for a purpose, gentlemen,' started Henry still choking.

'I was just going to tell you, Richard, as I wasn't expecting Thomas to be here, so I'm glad I have you both together. I am not well, gentlemen, and the doctors tell me that I will not see Christmas. I have no time for doctors but I presume that, with the way I am feeling, they may be right. Who knows? Anyway, I have no family to leave all the estate to, and I certainly do not want to see our present useless government get a penny of it. I have talked to my legal people and everything is looking quite straightforward.

When you went back to Ireland, Thomas, you signed over the estate to me for a considerable life-long income for yourself, and decreed that Richard would be the estate manager for life. I see that there is no reason, then, that this cannot continue after I die, except that I will sign the estate back to you, the rightful owner. I am sure that's what my brother would have wanted me to do with it.' He started to cough loudly, and Thomas jumped up and got him a glass of water.

Richard, looked on in disbelief. Without speaking a word, he suddenly jumped up and poured himself a large glass of whiskey. 'Would anyone else like one of these?' he asked, excitedly.

'No thank you. We're both fine at this time of the day, and you don't need it either.' Thomas took the glass from him and put it back on the sideboard. Just then, Ann walked in.

'This is my wife, Ann, Sir Henry.' Richard proudly introduced her.

'You're a very lucky young man, Richard. Pleased to meet you, Ann.'

'Please don't get up, Sir,' replied Ann, realising that he was having difficulty standing.

'Richard has told me some of your family history and I would love to hear more of your story sometime,' she said kindly.

'So you shall, my dear, if my nephew allows me to stay tonight. Then perhaps we can talk more at dinner. Now I must take a rest, folks, as I have been in the coach for four hours.'

Richard pulled out all the stops and dinner was a more formal occasion than had been seen in the house for a very long time. Sir Henry and Ann sat beside each other and he told her all about how he and his brother had been born into inherited wealth. He never asked her what her background was. Richard had never told her the story of the estate, and it made no difference to her who owned what as she felt that she was out of place as a working girl anyway and didn't deserve such a luxurious life style.

Dinner was a happy event, until Thomas made a statement that shocked them all.

'If I am to be the owner of the family estate again,' he started, standing up, 'I intend to do something which has been on my mind for some time.'

The others looked up with alarm. 'Edward my brother-in-law, who tried to kill me, has been in prison for sixteen years. I think that is long enough for any man to be put away. I propose to write to a senior magistrate and ask that he be released from prison on condition that he never comes near this house again. I believe that everyone in life deserves a second chance, and I hold no grudge against him. I also propose that we sell a small section of the estate, perhaps about two hundred acres, and give it to him as a gift from his father and uncle.'

Sir Henry stared at Thomas for a long time. Then said slowly, 'Now I can see why my niece thought you were the kindest man she had ever met. I believe my brother would be very proud of you, Thomas, and I approve of your plan – but with some reservations.'

Richard was speechless. He did not like the plan at all.

Chapter 20

The next morning, after breakfast, they said their sad goodbyes to Sir Henry as they all knew they would never see him again. Thomas gave him a big hug, which took him by surprise, and told him that the estate would always stay in his family and be looked after. As the coach pulled away from the front door, Henry wiped a few tears from his eyes and, after he left, Thomas, Richard and Ann stood in silence, staring at the empty driveway.

Thomas turned to Richard and said calmly. 'I need a new person to run my estate.'

The colour drained from his face and he turned to Thomas with a look of shock and betrayal in his face. He could hardly speak. 'I don't understand, Thomas,' he stuttered, 'I thought you were pleased at the way I have run it.'

'I am very pleased,' replied Thomas, smiling. 'That's the problem. I think you are now wasted here as there's very little to be done, apart from maintenance. I don't want you to sitting here idle all day long"

Richard was now looking a bit anxious at what was coming next.

'I was lying in bed thinking last night, and I have a plan. I need you to come to Ireland and help me set up a new business or two in a city nearby called Derry. My country has been through a hard time, but it's starting to emerge from its sadness and I believe the time is ripe for new industry to help it prosper once again. My trip to America was a complete failure and I don't want to make another mistake at home.' He paused and took hold of Richard's shoulders.

'There is no other person on this earth that I could trust to help me start a business, and I believe that it would be good for Ann to get away from this area and start again where no one will ever know of her past.'

For the first time since they met, Thomas watched Richard's eyes fill with tears. 'Besides, living in this mansion does not become you.'

Thomas gave him a hug and then pulled back to hear his answer. 'Well what do you think?'

'I cannot think of a better plan. I just don't understand how you always have solutions to other people's problems. It's as if you have a direct line to God or something.'

Thomas smiled and patted him on the back, 'That's agreed then, my friend. It will take a bit of time to organise. I need you to take time and find a reliable person to run this estate, as it will finance our business at home. I will build or buy you a house near mine which will take a wee while. If we plan for you to move in, say March or April, then it will give me time to see what industry to start.'

'I would need to ask Ann about that. What do you think, Ann?' he asked, turning to his wife.

'I will go where you go, Richard. I will never leave you again,' Ann answered, smiling.

'You and Mary got on well, Ann, while you stayed with us last year. I'm sure you would be good for each other,'

'And now I must return home. I know I said I would be here for two weeks, but my work here is done and I must try and change my tickets,' said Thomas.

The three of them hugged, and Richard said, 'I need the glass of whiskey I poured yesterday.' They all laughed and walked back into the house.

After lunch Thomas told them he had one last thing to do before he would head back to Ireland. He didn't tell Richard and Ann where he was going but said he wanted to go there by horse rather than carriage.

Thomas arrived at the local jail where Edward was incarcerated and tied the horse to a post at the front door.

'I am Thomas Sweeney. I own the Shrewsbury estate.' Thomas announced, to the warden.

'I want to see Edward Lewis, son of the late Lord Shrewsbury,' he said, trying to put on a posh English accent. The warden closed the hatch and went away for about five minutes.

The man came back and opened the door. 'You have ten minutes, but if the prisoner doesn't want to see you, then you will have to leave.'

Thomas thanked him as he was led down a dingy corridor that led to a flight of stone stairs. It was cold, and smelled more like a farm shed than a place where people were being kept. They came to a long row of cell doors. After walking past six doors, the warden stopped and banged on a cell door. The prisoner was lying asleep on an old hair mattress and the stench nearly made Thomas sick. 'Prisoner Lewis, get up, you have a visitor,' the warden barked, and then left them to it. 'You have ten minutes,' he snapped.

Thomas didn't recognise Edward as he stumbled up from his bed. He was bent over, his clothes were filthy and he had a full length beard. He shuffled to the door. 'Who are you?' he asked, peering closely at Thomas.

'I am the man you tried to kill by shooting me in the forest sixteen years ago.' Thomas stated.

Edward examined him closely for a few seconds to make sure it was really him and then turned back to his bed. 'I don't want to see you,' he sneered, and shouted, 'Warden, get this man out of here!'

'I forgive you,' Thomas shouted back, hoping the warden wouldn't come back. Edward stopped and stood still, before he turned back to look at Thomas.

'Why?' he snarled. Thomas was quiet for a while as he quietly prayed that God would give him the right words to say.

'Because I do not believe you meant to kill me and that you have served enough time for your mistake.'

Edward stared at him with in disbelief.

'I suppose that useless father of mine sent you today, out of his guilt,' Edward sneered.

Thomas went quiet for a few seconds and took a deep breath. 'Edward, did no one tell you your father died fifteen years ago, not long after you came here?'

'Good,' he snarled.

'I don't believe you mean that. It was a judge who sent you here, not your father.' Thomas replied softly.

'My father hated me and loved you instead,' he said, raising his voice.

'Your father loved you Edward. It's just that you went out of your way to make sure he never showed it,' Thomas answered crossly. 'You were spoilt, but never realised it.'

Edward was silent and Thomas was hoping he hadn't just crossed the line.

'When I married your sister, Christina, I inherited the estate, and when she died it all became mine,' Thomas said softly again. Edward looked shocked and stood staring at him for a long time.

'What did you just say? Christina is dead?'

'She died having our first baby, Edward, a year after your father was killed. Did no one not tell you this?' Thomas asked. Edward just stared at the floor before turning back to Thomas.

'Why are you here then, Irishman?' he snarled.

'I am returning to my family in Ireland and I want to see you set free from here,' he said, staring into Edward's eyes through the door.

'I am in here for life. What can you do, and why would you do it anyway?' Edward sighed.

'I will write to the magistrate and ask him to release you into my care.'

'What?' shouted Edward 'What has possessed you to think that I would ever want anything from the man who stole my father's heart and his money?'

'I told you I forgive you and want to give you back some of what is yours,' Thomas said urgently, 'Look. I don't have much time, so listen to me closely if you want to live again,'

Thomas heard the warden's door open again. 'I'll ask the magistrate to release you into my care. You will then return to a small house and run part of the estate that we have made profitable again. You'll have a reasonable income for life, but you must decide now as I return to Ireland in the morning and you will have no way of contacting me.'

The warden appeared beside Thomas and shouted, 'Time's up. Prisoner, return to your bed.'

Thomas pleaded with the warden.'One second please. I need an answer from the prisoner.'

'You would do that for me even though I tried to kill you,' asked Edward, with tears in his eyes, as he turned to face Thomas.

'Yes, for your father's and sister's sake I would, but I need an answer now,' Thomas pleaded.

The warden said it was time to go and started to push Thomas away from the cell door.

'I will accept your offer then,' shouted Edward, as Thomas walked back along the corridor.

'I hope you will hear soon, Edward,' Thomas called, as he was shown the front door.

'Where were you all afternoon?' asked Richard, when Thomas climbed down from his horse at the stables.

'I would tell you, but you wouldn't believe me, my friend,' Thomas smiled and headed for the house, 'Now, I think I might join you for that whiskey.'

Chapter 21

The journey home was uneventful. Thomas noticed, as he looked out of the windows of the endless train journeys, that the country was changing rapidly. In every town he went through were huge new factories being built and new towns and villages were springing up in isolated places. He thought about home in Ireland and how it seemed to get the advancements later than other parts of Britain. 'I'll change that,' he thought. 'It's time for my wee country to thrive again and forget about its sad past,'

On one of the trains he met a businessman who was opening a new clothes factory near Manchester. Thomas questioned him for the two hours while he was on the train as to what industry might do well in Ireland. He questioned everyone he met trying to get ideas to bring home.

John was waiting for him at his front gate, as the coach arrived from Derry.

'Good day, Thomas, how was your trip?' asked John as he took Thomas's bag from him.

'Extraordinary, John,' Thomas laughed, 'I could write a book about my week in England.'

'Life is always an adventure for you, sir, wherever you go. Perhaps you should go away more often.' John laughed.

'I'm thirty-seven. I reckon it's now time for me settle down,' Thomas sighed, as he started to walk up his long driveway. 'How's my family? I haven't been keeping in touch with them.'

'All good, sir, and will be very surprised and pleased to see you home early, and without any war wounds,' John smiled.

'I'm bringing Richard and Ann here to live with me,' Thomas started slowly. 'I'll need his help to start my next venture.'

John was very surprised and didn't reply straight away. 'Don't worry. He'll not replace you. I want to start a new business in Derry and I'll need you to keep running this estate,'

He seemed greatly relieved, 'I am sure he will be a big help to you, Thomas, having turned around your estate in England to be so profitable.'

'I wasted so much time in America, and the only good thing I learned is how not to treat people from other lands,' Thomas said, pausing to look at one of the bushes they had planted that was in full bloom. 'We have an opportunity to make this land great again, and we will need all the help we can get from anyone who wants to work, no matter where they are from or their skin colour.'

John looked at Thomas but said nothing. Eventually, they arrived at the house. Colleen saw them first and came running towards her father, 'Da! You're home! Yippee!' she shouted and jumped into his arms. Thomas held her close.

John left Thomas's bag inside the door and excused himself and Mary, hearing the noise, came running out to meet him. At dinner, they all wanted to hear about his trip to England and were pleased to hear that Thomas had found Ann and that they were coming to live nearby. Mary didn't ask Thomas about staying in the house as she knew Thomas would have found that very difficult. She left that till they were in bed together that night.

'Well, my love. How was it staying in your old house?' Mary asked, apprehensively.

Thomas thought for a long time as he lay with his arms around Mary. 'To be honest, it was very sad, as every part of the house held a different memory; some good, some not so good,' he sighed, lying back with his hands behind his head. 'Life is such a mystery, Mary. One minute you have something that seems very precious and the next minute it's gone. it's almost like a game of cat and mouse and you don't know what's around the next corner. If I have learnt anything in my short life it's to enjoy every day as if it's your last, as we have no way of knowing if it's.'

'God has a good plan for each one of us, but some times we spoil that plan by going off in the wrong direction,' said Mary.

'I know, just like I took us to America for my own selfish reasons and could have got all of us killed,' he sighed.

Mary just smiled and put her arm around him, 'Well, God made no mistake when he gave me my best friend as a husband, that was for sure.

Thomas stared thoughtfully at Mary and then whispered contentedly, 'Christina was not a mistake, my love. She was just part of my journey back to you.' He put the light out and they went to sleep.

Four months later

The Christmas of 1861 was cold in Donegal, and there was a heavy snowfall on Christmas Eve, which made the place look quite magical. Michael, Colleen and Charity had so much fun as they built snowmen and had snowball fights with Thomas. The grandmothers had arrived the day before, and Thomas had put them into a new house in their grounds, but never told them it was built especially for them. John, who had sent all his staff home to be with their families, was invited to join them for the week, and he was glad of the rest. Richard and Ann had done the same in England and they were spending Christmas in Yorkshire with Richard's parents.

As they all sat down for Christmas dinner, it seemed a very long way from the year that they all had been through. Thomas sat and looked at them all and, for the first time in his life, felt that he had achieved something good. He secretly gave thanks to God for Lord Shrewsbury and Christina, who changed his life for ever. He reminisced about meeting the surveyor nineteen years before on a hill only miles away from Greencastle and how the one day's work changed his destiny from poverty to wealth. He remembered the days with Mary watching the sea at Kinnego Bay and the tragedy of watching both their parents drown. The sadness of hearing Mary's story of hardship in New York and her rescue by John, funded by the English landlord, Sir William. He felt both contented and sad that life was so full of good and bad but that, right now, all was good.

When they all had finished eating, Thomas stood up to make a speech. 'This is a great and happy day for my family but I'm sad that not everyone we love can be with us today, so we remember them, and also realise that, without many of them, we wouldn't be having such a happy Christmas. I would like to welcome John here today and to thank him for his incredible dedication to our family. I wish him well in the next year and hope he finds a good wife at long last.' They all laughed, and John blushed, before Thomas continued. 'I would also like to toast my amazing Mary and our two incredible children for putting up with my crazy life and for being the best I could ever dream of. To Bridget and Rose who have had to endure far too much pain, and

Mary's sister, Martha, who I believe will sing us a song later. I would also like to welcome Charity into our family. I pray that 1862 will be the year that God will bring health and contentment to everyone here, and that our wee island of Ireland will return to good times.' They all stood and raised their glasses and applauded loudly.

After, they moved around the big roaring turf and wood fire to chat and listen to Martha sing traditional Irish songs, Thomas sat beside John and whispered 'Any good ideas for a business yet?'

'Derry is open to so much, Thomas, and has a great workforce that could do almost anything,' John started. 'In a few weeks time, on the first of January, two men called Harland and Wolff are opening a new ship-building yard in Belfast. They say it's going to be one of the biggest in the world and will employ thousands. It seems that heavy industry is going to boom, but also that the world has a shortage of good quality clothes manufacturers. William Scott, who died four years ago, had a very successful shirt making business in the city. His company is still doing very well selling shirts all over the world, and there are also some new companies. The railways are only starting here, and there could be a big opportunity there too. I would say that if you do some more research you would do well in any new business.'

'Richard will be here at the start of April, so by then, I want to have a good idea of what to start, but for now, let's enjoy the fun.'

Chapter 22

January started with a bad storm. The snow had gone just after Christmas, but now the winds were reaching hurricane force. Thomas had finally convinced their two mothers and Martha to move to the new house beside him.

He received a letter from the English magistrate informing him that it was possible that Edward's sentence could be reduced on account of his good behaviour in jail but that Thomas would have to also speak with the warden of the jail. Thomas was sad, as he thought it would be highly unlikely that he would allow that. He sent a letter to Edward explaining the situation, but never received a reply.

As soon as the storm was over Thomas decided that he would take a trip to Derry and spend a few days looking around to see what business he might start. He and Michael also sat down together every evening designing the new pier that they would build in the spring.

The storm lasted four days and did considerable damage to many parts of Donegal. Thomas rode into Moville on his horse and he was shocked to see much of the town centre had been destroyed. He met the mayor on the street as he stood surveying the damage. 'Daniel, the place is in terrible mess,' he said, coming up beside him.

'It's that,' he replied. 'I don't know how we'll put all this together again.'

'I will help, Daniel. Let me know how much it might cost to fix the square. I can't help every shop that's damaged, but I can fix a fair bit.'

Daniel was speechless and just stared at Thomas for a moment, 'You are mighty generous, Mr Sweeney! The people will be very grateful to you,' he stuttered.

'I would prefer if the people didn't know where the money came from, Daniel. Good day to you,' Thomas walked off.

As he was passing the post office, the postman ran out after him. 'Mr Sweeney, a telegram just came for you and I was about to deliver it to you but you'd better have it now, sir.'

'Thank you,' Thomas said as he quickly peeled it open.

'Ah no! It can't be,' Thomas said very sadly. 'It can't be! Thank you, postman,' he turned and walked very slowly towards his horse.

Mary was hanging clothes on the line at the side of the house when Thomas rode up the driveway. He stopped and shouted to her.

'What's wrong, Thomas? she asked, running over to the horse.

'Read this telegram that has just come from the prison warden who I asked to release Edward,' Thomas said, handing the telegram to Mary.

'Awe no! How very sad!'

They both looked at each other with questioning eyes.

'It says that Edward is dead but it doesn't say how. Do you think he may have killed himself?' Mary asked, sadly.

'I told him the magistrate said he couldn't release him and that I would have to apply to the warden. I guess he must have realised that the warden would never release him as they were always fighting.' Thomas dismounted his horse. 'I never thought he would do that.'

'He died knowing that you had forgiven him, my love, and maybe he repented of what he tried to do to you,' Mary said.

'That's good, but I was going to give him back a lot of what he had lost. Of course I could never give him back his his father and sister,' Thomas said sadly. 'I genuinely wanted him to recover, poor man.'

Mary came up and stroked Thomas's face.

'You did what God wanted you to do, and that is all that matters,' Mary said softly.

'Is it? Sometimes I still wonder if God on my side at all.'

'Don't ever doubt, Thomas. The reason you have such a soft heart is because God has given it to you.'

'Well if he has, then I wish he would stop breaking it,' Thomas said, as he walked the horse to the house.

The next day he got another telegram to say that Sir Henry had also died. Thomas just stared at the telegram and wondered if anyone had told him about his nephew, Edward. 'I hope not,' thought Thomas. 'He had too much sadness in his lifetime.'

Thomas rode over to John and asked him to go to the city with him. He was quiet as they caught the taxi coach to Derry. They both stared quietly out at River Foyle as they made the seventeen mile journey. John didn't want to interrupt Thomas's thoughts, as Mary had told him that he had received two telegrams with sad news.

'How did you ever find Mary, John, in a city as big as New York?' Thomas asked suddenly.

John was taken back at suddenly being reminded of something he had mostly forgotten. 'I would say,' he stated slowly, 'that I didn't find her, but God did.'

Thomas looked at him with curiosity, 'Talk to me, my friend. I need to hear that God did something good, for a change.'

John was shocked and a bit embarrassed. 'I thought you were a believer. I'm surprised that you find it hard to believe that it was God, not I, that rescued Mary.'

'I've had so much sadness recently that I am only clinging lightly to my trust in God, but maybe your story might help me.'

John reiterated the full story of how he found Mary, but included more detail this time. It did, indeed, seem miraculous how he had found her in a city as big as New York.

Thomas was silent and he had tears in his eyes, 'So you see, Thomas. I didn't find Mary; God took me to her.'

'I never heard the full story from Mary. Thank you, my friend, for doing what you thought was right. I needed to hear that today.'

'We only think our lives are in our own hands, but God is ultimately in control,' John said, with confidence,' as he pointed out the window. 'We're here now.'

Thomas and John spent the next two days walking around the city of Derry looking at existing shops and businesses. They walked up onto the historic walls that looked out in every direction, looking for inspiration. There were two new shirt factories and quite a number of small breweries. The shops on Shipquay Street and Bishop Street seemed to cater for most needs of the city folk. The last place they walked to before heading home was the quays, where all the ships docked. Most of the ships were unloading coal or grain, and there was a new passenger ship that now went to Glasgow. Thomas walked silently, noticing all the hustle and bustle, and then stopped and looked down the river. 'You said, John, that a new shipbuilding dock was being opened in Belfast.'

'Yes, by two men, who are calling the place after their family names, Harland and Wolff.'

'So why could we not make smaller boats here?' Thomas asked, smiling.

'The city already has a shipbuilding business which builds large ships.'

'Small cargo ships or large fishing boats, John. No one is making them in Ireland. They are being bought from across the sea,' Thomas said, confidently. 'Boats – my da loved boats and I love them as well. So why not build them? It's just an idea - or maybe some other heavy industry?'

They turned and started walking back towards the city centre where they would get their taxi home. John wasn't convinced, but decided to say nothing.

On the journey home, Thomas noticed that John was unusually pensive, 'So, John, a penny for your thoughts, my friend. It's not like you to be so quiet.'

John smiled and continued looking out the carriage window at the River Foyle. 'Mary's sister Martha – she's very pretty,'

Thomas was shocked at first. Then after a while he smiled, 'Yes she is, very pretty – and not married yet.' John was embarrassed and just smiled at Thomas, before turning back to look out the window.

Chapter 23

3 months later

Spring came early that year and the sun was shining through the kitchen window as they all sat at the table for breakfast. Thomas was reading a pile of letters and documents when he announced, 'I've told Richard to sell part of the estate in England, folks.'

'That's a big decision! Why now?' Mary replied, as she spooned eggs onto the children's plates.

'I've no choice, Mary,' Thomas said, getting up from the table, 'The unexpected death duties from Sir Henry mean I have no choice. I have enough money to pay them now, but it would then take the estate maybe five years to recover that amount, and besides, the sale will give us the extra capital I need to start my new business here.'

'Will there be enough income from a smaller estate to keep Richard and Ann as well?' Mary asked, concerned.

'We'll have enough income for us all and more from my new venture,' Thomas said, putting his arm around her shoulder.

'Did we make money on our New York house?' Mary was worried.

'No, we lost a small amount, but not too bad, considering there's a war on and we were not well liked there.' Thomas laughed.

'It's not good to live off money in a bank. We need a secure income in these days,' Mary said, as she gathered up some plates for washing.

'I know, Mary. Richard will be here soon and will help me start my new business,' Thomas said as he headed for the door. Mary wasn't totally convinced.

Thomas rode over to visit John. He was in the front garden showing one of his workmen how he wanted the new garden designed. 'Morning, Thomas. What brings you here on this great spring morning?'

'Richard and Ann are arriving next week, and I wanted to talk to you about the estate. Some of the changes that we have made have been on his advice and I don't want you to feel awkward if, when he comes, he makes some more suggestions,' Thomas said, dismounting from his horse. 'We will need to make this place pay for itself, as we no longer get rent from our tenants, and it will probably mean a lot of changes.'

John looked at Thomas thoughtfully. He knew he was a clever and honourable man. 'This is your home, sir, and I am only here to look after it, so I will be very happy to do whatever you please.'

Thomas stared at the new fountain. 'I bought this estate with revenge in my heart, and it was with the intention of making Sir William and Maud homeless after what they did to my mother. I had a major change of heart due to a number of circumstances, and sadly we are here now today and they are no longer here to enjoy it. Strange how life works – sometimes not.'

'They were exceptionally kind to me and I will never forget them, and making this place great again will be my way of thanking them, and you,' John assured Thomas.

Just then they heard Mary screaming, as she ran towards them. 'Thomas, come quickly! It's Michael,' she cried.

Thomas ran and grabbed her arms. 'What's wrong?'

'I searched for Michael all over the house and couldn't find him, and as I was running around the garden I noticed the boat's gone. I ran to the shore and can see the boat a long way down the river, and it looks like Michael's trying to row back but can't cope with the strong tide.'

Thomas jumped on his horse, 'Leave Mary home again, John. I 'll see if anyone can help me in Greencastle.' 'Stupid boy!' he muttered, as he galloped down the driveway.

It took Thomas twenty minutes to ride to the Greencastle harbour where most of the fishermen were sitting in the sun mending their nets.

'I have an emergency! Do any of you have a free boat?' he shouted, as he jumped off his horse.

They all looked at him for a minute before one of the older men said 'What's the problem, sir?'

'My son has gone out rowing in my boat on his own and he's only fifteen. He can't row against the tide. He'll soon drift out to sea!' Thomas said, in a panic.

'Joe has a small sail boat there. I'll see if he can help you,' the man said calmly. He disappeared into the fish processing shed at the top of the pier, appearing a few minutes later with a young man wearing waders. 'Where's your boy now'? the young fisherman asked.

'My wife said he was well down the river from out house, so he should be fairly close to us by now.' Thomas replied.

They all climbed onto the harbour wall to look out on the sea. 'There's the boat over there.' said the young fisherman. 'We need to set sail straight away.'

Thomas felt sick as, once again, his memory of nearly drowning with his father came rushing back to him.

The two men sailed speedily towards the small fishing boat. Their boat was twenty five feet long and had one small sail in the middle and an extended rudder arm at the back. They quickly loosened the ropes and pulled the sail up, 'Not much room for you, but you can come with us if you want,' the older fisherman shouted. Thomas jumped into the boat as it pulled away from the pier.

The wind was off the land, which meant the small boat picked up speed very quickly, and it only took twenty minutes to reach it. He gasped in surprise when he saw it was Charity, alone, in the boat, but just then the young fisherman shouted, 'Someone's hanging on to the back of the boat.'

Thomas was about to jump into the sea when the fisherman stopped him. 'Let us do it, sir. We don't want the boat to capsize.'

They quickly pulled the sail down and, using one of their oars, pulled the rowing boat next to their boat so they could lift Michael out of the water. He was choking and spitting up water. Thomas grabbed him and pulled him into the boat. 'Sorry, Da,' Michael choked. Thomas said nothing but just held him close and stroked his hair. The young fisherman helped Charity climb onto his boat. She was the first black person he had ever seen and it was hard for him to hide his fascination.

Back at the harbour, the men helped the three of them out of the boat. 'Maybe he should see a doctor,' the old man said. 'The sea is ice cold at this time of year and he'll need warmed up slowly.'

'Thank you so much, men,' Thomas said, still shaking. 'Please let me know how I can repay you for your kindness.'

'No payment needed, my friend,' the man said. 'Very glad we got to them in time. We'll see to your boat for you.'

Thomas put Michael onto his horse and he and Charity led him back home. No one spoke.

Mary and John were waiting by the beach when Thomas appeared leading the horse with Michael slumped on it. 'Get him inside quickly, Mary. He's half frozen and needs to be warmed up slowly.' Charity was crying, and ran to Mary. John lifted Michael down from the horse and carried him into the house where they stripped him of his wet clothes and put a blanket around him. He sat huddled by the living room fire. Thomas looked at the other two and they silently agreed to say nothing for now.

'Would you stay for dinner, John?' Mary asked kindly. 'It'll be ready in an hour, and Martha will be arriving from over the hill any time now.'

John felt his cheeks going red, but agreed to stay. 'Thank you. I'll go and put the horse in the stable for Thomas.'

Thomas had left the horse to graze and it was making its way towards Mary's plants. 'Whoa, boy,' John said softly to the horse, 'That's not a tasty dinner for you. Come till I get you some proper food.'

'Who are you talking to, John?' asked Martha, as she strolled up the driveway.

John was surprised to see Martha and, yet again, his heart jumped at the sight of such a beautiful woman. 'There aren't many people to talk to round here, Martha, so myself and the horse were having a discussion about eating your sister's plants,' John laughed, moving the horse towards her.

Well, I'm here now,' she laughed 'and I can make better conversation than that thing.'

'Right so, ma'am. Let me put her in the stables and I'll be back.'

'No, I'll come with you.' She left her bag by the fence and followed John to the stables at the back of the house, with a big smile on her face.

To John's surprise, Martha suddenly began pouring out her heart to him. 'Can I tell you something that's been bothering me, John?' John nodded. 'When I was young, I was told that I was slow,' Martha said, solemnly, as she patted the horse. 'I believed it for a while, as it meant I could have my life to myself, and sometimes I wasn't held accountable when I was naughty. I guess I was a bit naughty but it meant I could dream of a different life. When Mary went to New York I was fifteen and realised I would have to help me Ma, so I grew up. That was very boring, but I had to do it for their sakes. I only dreamed of one thing that has yet to come to pass.'

John was stunned at Martha's honesty and that she confided in him so freely. 'I've known you since you were seventeen. I always thought that you were, not only beautiful, but also very mysterious, and I never thought for one moment that you were slow,' he said, staring into her eyes.

'You haven't asked me what I dreamed of.' Martha walked to the stable door, laughing, 'I'll tell you soon.'

John watched her walk out the door. He wanted to run after her but stopped himself.

'I love you Martha,' he whispered to himself, 'but how will I ever tell you?'

Just then he heard Thomas calling.

Dinner that evening was quieter than usual, as Thomas and Mary were waiting for Michael and Charity to tell their story of taking the boat, but they both stayed silent. Colleen was the only one who was full of chat about some new boys who had come to her school. John and Martha sat opposite each other and smiled nervously at each other.

'I am very glad you gave us a new house,' Martha started, smiling. 'I never thought I would ever leave Kinnego but it's very handy here and the neighbours are nice.'

John looked at her, knowingly.

'We'll have more neighbours next week, Martha, when Richard and Ann arrive,' Mary chipped in.

'Oh that's nice, but they'll be living on our land and so they won't really be neighbours.' Martha laughed as she got up from the table.

'There'll be a few changes around here,' Thomas said. 'All for the better though.'

The sun was starting to set when Thomas walked out of the front door. He saw Michael sitting down at the pier, where the boat had been kept. He sat down beside him and then said quietly.

'So what was that wee adventure about, son?'

Michael stared out to sea. 'I'm fifteen now, Da, and I just wanted to be like you and Granda.'

He stopped and looked down at the ground, 'I'm sorry, Da, for giving you a fright. I thought I could row the boat like you do, but the outgoing tide caught me and I couldn't row against it.'

Thomas laughed, as he put his arm around his shoulders, 'I presume you were trying to impress Charity, son, as well.'

Michael blushed and said nothing.

'It was a good lesson, son, as you can never trust the sea. If your ma hadn't noticed you, the tide would have taken you out to sea. It doesn't bear thinking about.'

'Will we get your boat back, Da?' Michael asked, sheepishly.

'It's already sorted, son. The fisherman said he would tow it back when they go out fishing tomorrow. Anyway I wasn't worried about the boat, only you, son.'

Michael smiled at his Da.

'By the way, what happened?' Thomas asked. 'How did you manage to land in the water?'

'One of the oars came off the rowlock and fell into the water. I panicked and tried to reach over the back of the boat to grab it and I fell in. Charity threw the stern rope. If it wasn't for her, I would have drowned. I was very scared, Da. I couldn't have held on much longer.'

'We need to thank her, son. We both have had miracles happen to us, so I guess we still have a purpose here on earth. Let's go for a wee walk, son.' Thomas pulled Michael up by the arm and they both walked down the drive.

Just then, Charity came out of the house and stood staring at the sea. Michael left his dad and hurried to talk to her. When he got to the door, she turned and looked at him with tears in her eyes. 'I thought I was going to lose you, Michael,' she said softly, looking into his eyes.

'I owe my life to you, Charity. That was some distance you threw the rope! I just don't know how you did it.'

'You mean, "not bad for a girl",' she laughed, with a hint of sarcasm.

'If that boat hadn't come, I couldn't have held on for another minute. I'm sorry for putting your life in danger, and thank you for not letting go.' Michael was awkward now and moved from foot to foot.

'I couldn't bear the thought of losing you, even if you are headstrong and want to go and fight in wars,' she said, smiling. She moved closer to him, which made him even more nervous.

'Do you think you could be happy here,' Michael asked timidly, 'I mean, being from a different country and all?'

'You mean, because I'm black, and no one here has ever seen a black person before?' She came right up to face him.

'I would just want you to be happy, Charity, even though local people would talk. I more than owe you my life. I feel deeply about you.'

'And me for you, Michael, and yes, I believe I could be happy here.' She kissed him gently, but then got embarrassed.

Just then Mary came out the door looking for Colleen.

Chapter 24

Richard and Ann arrived on a sunny Saturday afternoon. Thomas, Mary and John were waiting for them at the front gate. They had hired two coaches in Derry to bring all their small luggage, while a transport company would bring the big items later.

'Welcome to Ireland, my friend,'

'If your local ale is not up to my standard', laughed Richard 'I will be on the next ship home.'

He went over and hugged Mary and shook hands with John.

'We have a drink here called Guinness. It'll beat your watery English ale any day.'

'We'll see about that. Now where is this majestic house you have for us?

Thomas started walking towards a new entrance they had made two hundred yards past the their driveway. 'This will be about a tenth of the size of the house you have been living in, but it will mean less staff,' Thomas joked, 'But sure it's only the two of you, unless you're planning to start a family.'

Richard stopped and turned to Thomas 'Well, actually, we were going to tell you later. Ann's expecting.'

'Great news, Ann!' Mary said, smiling. 'We need some new life about here. When are you due?'

'Just before Christmas,' Ann said quietly, 'all being well.'

They turned the corner and Thomas said, proudly, 'Well, what do you think?'

Richard and Ann stopped and stared at their beautiful new home that Thomas had built for them.

It was a long white house built of stone and was the first house in Donegal to have a slate roof.

It had three floors with a small conservatory built at the northern end overlooking the River Foyle.

'It's simply magnificent, Thomas. I had no idea the house was going to be as perfect as this. Thank you so much, my friend.'

'Well I could hardly have my best friend living in a hovel when you have come from one of the biggest houses in West England,' Thomas laughed, patting him on the back. 'Wait till you see the inside.'

Michael, Colleen, and Charity came running up behind them to see their new neighbours.

'Who is this young lady, then?' Richard asked, looking at Charity.

'This is Charity, from New York. She's come to live with us here in Ireland,' Mary broke in, smiling. 'She lost her daddy and was going to be living on her own at seventeen in New York, so we agreed she might find a better life here in Ireland.'

'And so you will,' rejoined Ann, as she went over to Charity and took her by the arm to lead her into the new house.

Thomas asked Richard quietly, 'What about the estate?'

'Some good and bad news there, but I trust it will work out well. The good news is that I found a very clever manager to run it. The bad news is, that he can only stay for a year, which may mean I will have to go back to England as the estate cannot run on its own and I wouldn't want the house to be lying vacant. Thomas looked at Richard with concern before patting him on the back and replying,'Well sure, my friend, there can be many changes in a year, so let's see what way the wind blows. I made a big mess of things in America and now I just want to live a simple life again with a small business to keep me busy.'

John came over to the two of them as they were about to go in the front door. 'Excuse me, Thomas, but one of my workers heard some unusual news this morning in Moville.'

Thomas and Richard stopped. 'What happened?'

'They said a strange looking man with a long coat and hat with a funny accent was asking where an old friend, called Thomas Sweeney, lived. The locals didn't like the look of him, so no one told him anything.'

Thomas looked worried, and moved nervously, but said nothing. Richard took his arm and they both went into the house. 'Thanks, John,' Thomas called back. Then said quietly said to Richard, 'That sounds strange, doesn't it?'

Richard could see Thomas was afraid, so made light of it. 'Probably a tax man checking you out, Thomas. I wouldn't worry about it.'

Mary invited them all round for dinner that evening and as it was so warm she spread everything out on a big table at the front of the house. Michael came up to his da while no one was watching and quietly asked him if he could take Charity for a walk along the shore to Greencastle. Thomas looked at him for a minute, then agreed as long as they kept away from the boat. Colleen spent most of the evening talking to Ann, and Mary could see that they could become good friends. John sat down beside Mary and started talking about how Martha was showing very direct signs that she was interested in more than friendship with him.

'She's thirty, and I can not speak for my sister,' Mary said gently.

'I know, but I'm forty and neither of us have had relationships before. I'm nervous about becoming close to someone. What if she has the wrong motives?' John sighed.

'What motives would they be now?' Mary asked, sympathetically.

'She would make any man a great wife, but I don't know if she loves me or just feels sorry for me.'

'Ask her, John.' Mary got up from her chair, 'She's coming up the driveway now.'

John jumped off his seat. 'No, I must go. I must check on my staff.'

'Do you love her?' Mary asked, suddenly.

John nearly choked on his glass of wine that he was finishing quickly, 'That's a very personal question,' he stuttered and then lowered his voice, 'Yes I probably do.'

'Well,' Mary turned to go into the house with some plates, 'Don't let it pass you. A door can close very quickly, you know.'

Just then Martha arrived 'Good evening, John. Don't tell me you're leaving already,' she smiled.

'I have a few things to sort out back at my house, ma'am, and it's probably better that I see to them, 'John said, as he bowed in front of her.

'Good. Then I'll come and help you,' Martha said, taking him by the arm, 'I wouldn't want to see an Irish bachelor walking down the lane on his own. You never know who might snatch him.' John was mortified that Mary heard this and turned to her for help, but Mary was laughing so hard she had to run into the house. 'Do you know, Martha, maybe the things could wait a wee while and perhaps we could walk the other direction along the shore.'

'Right so, master,' Martha replied as she pulled him around and they walked arm in arm towards the sea.

There was silence between them for a long time as they enjoyed the evening walk, with the sea on their right and mature trees lining the path on their left. They could see the small fishing boats returning to the harbour at Greencastle about a mile away.

'So, John,' started Martha suddenly, 'I'm a plain and simple girl who loves the good things in life, and I can never understand people who complicate things. I like to help my ma with the chickens and baking scones. I love to walk by the sea, and I don't bother much about what is happening to our country or world, so long as life is fairly good here.'

'That's a very good and brave way of looking at life,' John replied, slowly looking down at the sand. 'I wish my life was so simple, but unfortunately I have responsibilities to other people, and so much of my life is spent in pleasing others.'

They both stopped and looked at each other, before Martha said, smiling, 'Ah sure, we would make a good couple then, wouldn't we?' She paused, and smiled. 'You could look after the complicated things in life and I could look after the simple things.'

John didn't know what to say as he always thought it was up to the man to make advances to a woman, and now Martha was openly suggesting they get together. He stared at her, then took her hands in his and smiled, 'Would you ever think of marrying me then, Martha?'

'Of course I will,' she whispered, shyly. 'I can't think of anything I'd want more.'

They embraced and then kissed passionately. After a while they turned and walked hand in hand back towards the house. They were a short distance away when a man walked down from the path onto the beach in front of them. He was wearing a long winter coat, which John thought was strange for a summer evening. He also had a hat, the type of which John remembered from his stay in New York. They walked towards each other until the man stopped and touched his hat as a salute.

'Good evening, folks,' the man started, in an American accent. 'It's a very pleasant evening for a walk by the sea.'

John was alarmed, as the man fitted the description of the person who was asking for Thomas. 'Are you lost sir?' he asked tentatively.

'I was told Thomas Sweeney lived along here somewhere. Would you happen to know which house I might find him in?' the man asked.

'Not in these parts but you might try up the coast,' John answered slowly. 'May I ask why you need to find him?'

'An old friend,' the man replied, as he turned and walked away. 'I'm sure I'll find him eventually'

Martha was about to join in, but thought better of it. Instead, she said quietly to John, 'Why did you lie, John? Sure the house is just around the corner.'

'I'm sorry, Martha, but there is something not right about that man. Why would an American be looking for Thomas unless he means him harm. We need to go and warn him now.'

They both walked quickly back to the house, holding hands, and found Thomas and Colleen sorting through some old fishing nets that he was going to repair.

'An American man was looking for you on the beach, Thomas. I told him you didn't live here,' John said, out of breath.

Thomas looked at John and then told Colleen to go and help her mother. 'That's very strange, unless it's something to do with us adopting Charity. We didn't have all the paperwork completed before we left and I took a chance bringing her on the ship without her papers.'

'He didn't look like an official. He looked more like one of the gangsters I saw in New York,'

Thomas shrugged his shoulders and picked up the nets.

Chapter 25

After breakfast Thomas announced that he was going on horseback to Moville. He had promised the local people that he would help repair the town centre after the bad storm. It was another warm day, so Mary was busy trying to organise the three teenagers to do something useful.

Thomas went out the back door and across the yard to the stables. His black mare was whinnying, with her head over the half door. 'I know, I know, girl. It's alright. We'll soon be on the road,' Thomas said, stroking the horse's face. Just then, he felt a hard metal object press against the back of his head.

'Don't make a sound or I'll shoot you,' the American said.

Thomas froze. 'What do you want?' he asked, nervously.

'I am taking you back to New York where you will be court martialled and executed for treason, Captain Sweeney,' the man said.

'How can I be court martialled when I never joined the army?' Thomas retorted angrily.

'Explain that to my chief when you get there. Now get your two horses out without making a sound,' he barked.

Thomas opened the stable door. 'You'll never get away with this, Thomas threatened. How do expect to get me on the ship to America when everyone knows who I am?'

'I've booked us on a ship from Limerick. No one will know you there.' The man pointed the gun at Thomas, 'If you make one false move I will kill you, so do not turn round.'

Thomas brought the two horses out and tied them to a bar while he lifted the saddles to put on their backs. He began to realise that this man might just do what he said and he started to slow down in hope that one of the family would come out to the stable. Tightening the girths on both saddles, he stood back, waiting for his next instruction.

'Why did you do it, Captain?' the American asked, with a softer tone.

'Do what?' Thomas answered sharply.

'Betray the Union Army by helping the Greycoats.'

'I was captured by the Greycoats and they only let me go because I showed them how to use the new Winchester rifle. They would have worked it out themselves eventually so I didn't help them much.'

'We lost a lot of men,' the American said, sadly.

'You would have lost them anyway as they walked into a place that had no cover, and no matter which side had better weapons, it was always going to be bad anyway,' Thomas answered. There was silence for a while while Thomas tightened the girth on one of the horses.

'Turn around, Captain,' the American said.

Slowly and cautiously, Thomas turned around.

'Lieutenant O'Hare! What are you doing here?' Thomas exclaimed.

'I was sent to Ireland to bring you back to New York.'

'To be honest, right now though, I'm not so sure I'm prepared to do that.' O'Hare put the gun back in his pocket.

Thomas gave a cautious sigh of relief and looked apprehensively at O'Hare. He tied the two horses onto the rail.

'I'm glad to hear that because I have no intention of ever leaving Ireland again.'

'That may be so, but I'll never be able to return to America unless I bring you with me,' the Lieutenant sighed, so I guess we are both in the same boat.'

O'Hare moved to Thomas and handed him his gun. 'You could shoot me now and that would solve a lot of problems,' he ventured. Thomas took his gun and threw it out the door into the long grass. 'What part of Ireland are you originally from, Alfred?'

'Cork,' O'Hare sat on the milking stool.

'Any family there?'

'One or two, if they're still alive after the famine,' O'Hare looked at the ground and sighed.

Just then, Mary and Michael came out the back door and walked over to Thomas.

'Look who's here, Mary,' Thomas said, as he patted the horses and put them back in the stalls.

'Oh my goodness! Lieutenant O'Hare! What on earth are you doing here?'

O'Hare just looked down, embarrassed. Thomas answered for him, 'It's a long story, Mary. Maybe he could tell us over a cup of tea.'

They all walked back to the house.

No one asked O'Hare why he had come to visit and they all seemed more interested in how the American Civil War was going. After an hour he began to excused himself.

'Will you go back, Alfred?' Thomas asked, as he walked down the driveway with him.

O'Hare stopped and turned to Thomas, 'I believe you're right, Thomas. There's no need for this war, and a lot of people are going to die for a cause that's not so clear cut any more. I should have remained a policeman for another few years but I'm free now and can never go back. Ireland is my homeland and it's time to start a new life again here. He shook Thomas's hand.

'Sorry for scaring you, back there, but I had no real intention of taking you back.'

'You're a good man, Alfred. I wish you well in the next chapter of your life and hope you find some family in Cork.'

2 months later

The wedding was a grand affair, and most likely the biggest event in the area for many years.

Thomas and Mary said no expense should be spared and it was held at the front of John's estate in the beautiful gardens. Invitations went out to all the locals in Greencastle and Moville and there was a great turn-out from among the community. The food was served on long wooden tables, and there were special events laid on for all the children. Many locals commented that it was like one of the old harvest fairs that used to be held before the famine.

John was dressed in formal wear and looked like he was the lord of the manor. Martha wore a traditional white wedding dress, but it was the very latest fashion brought in from Dublin. Richard and Ann were given the job of welcoming and entertaining guests, and Bridget and Rose were guests of honour, seated at a grand table covered in white linen tablecloths. Only Thomas noticed Michael and Charity sitting hand in hand by the fountain.

When the feasting was over it was time for the speeches. Thomas stood up and started, 'This is one of the happiest days of my life, friends, and I thank so many of you for coming. Many of you may not have heard, but Mary owes her life to this wonderful man, John, so it gives me great pleasure in asking you to toast John and my sister-in-law, Martha, on this special day.

For our wonderful families and friends, may I pray that this summer will be the start of a happier time in our land. I have prospered by the hand of God, and not on my own, and I pray that you will too. Some of you may have noticed that we brought back a young lady with us from America. It was our intention to adopt her, but I see today that we might not have to adopt her. Everyone laughed, and Michael and Charity nearly fell under the table. 'A toast then, to John and Martha.' He looked round and smiled at Mary, 'And to our next adventure!'